Flight 800

Dan Fulani

Spectrum Books Limited
Ibadan · Owerri · Kaduna · Lagos

Published by
Spectrum Books Limited
Sunshine House
1, Emmanuel Alayande Street
Oluyole Industrial Estate
P.M.B. 5612
Ibadan, Nigeria

in association with
Safari Books (Export) Limited
Bel Royal House
Hilgrove Street
St. Helier, Jersey
Channel Islands, UK

Europe and USA Distributor
African Books Collective Ltd.,
The Jam Factory,
27 Park End Street,
Oxford OX1, 1HU, UK

© Dan Fulani, 1983

First Published 1983

Reprinted 1996

ISBN 0-946480-04-4

Printed by Rolasesi Printers, Ibadan

To the real Queen, Charlie's friend.

Chapter One

The girl put her hands on her large unshapely hips, puffed out a chest which was nothing less than massive and stared hard at Pius Shale.

'My name, Mr Shale, is Queen. As I told you, Queen, is my name.' Pius Shale stared at his visitor, running his eye up and down a figure which although possessed by a female of no more than twenty-nine, resembled to his not inexperienced eye that of a singularly well-proportioned male.

Pius had already concluded that this good lady had no need of a man to look after her. She was clearly quite capable of looking after herself in every way. Having reached this conclusion, he was therefore taken aback by her next statement.

'Mr Shale,' she said in a voice which rasped like a rusty saw, 'I need help.'

Having recovered from the shock that a girl who was so powerfully built would ever ask for assistance, Pius pointed to the office chair which he and Bisi reserved for visitors, and said with extreme politeness, 'Won't you sit down, Miss Queen?'

'Missis,' came the curt response, 'and I prefer to stand.'

'I am sorry, Madam, I did not realise...'

'Why should you?' the girl cut in. 'Anyway, he has gone, vanished.'

'Who?'

'My husband, my man, my Mister Queen or Prince as his friends call him.'

Pius decided that the time had come to sit down himself, not because he was tired, not because he was reluctant to face a stand-up encounter with his formidable visitor. No, he wanted to sit down because it enabled him to flick on a switch concealed underneath the arm of his chair. A switch which would ensure that the whole of their subsequent conversation would be safely recorded on tape.

Something made him feel that Bisi would be interested in hearing his personal talk with Missis Queen.

'Where is your home?' asked Pius quietly.

The girl was busy groping in her handbag with a huge fist full of fingers, and what subsequently emerged was a large Havana cigar which she rammed between her teeth. The end was bitten off and spat on to the carpet. The reflection of the flame from her lighter lit up the large chunky and expensive jewellery which encompassed each of her fingers in a cluster of red, yellow and green. This girl had money.

'Bendel State.'

'Please, be precise.'

'Benin.'

'And your full name?'

'Missis Queen.'

'Please, madam, I must have a full name. We all have one even if we do not use it in public.'

The girl puffed herself up like a spitting cobra and then suddenly changing her mind, subsided.

'It would be too difficult for you to pronounce.'

'Try me'.

'Ogieriaxi.'

'Mhh,' said Pius quietly, 'I see what you mean. Anyway, if you spell it out for me I can write it down in my notebook.' Pius mentally kicked himself for not having had his notebook out earlier.

Missis Queen spelt out her surname and then with a verbal assault which resembled rapid machine gun fire, she spat out her statement.

'My man, Prince, has gone. One moment he is here, next moment he is not here. Gone, vanished, disappeared. Not that I am surprised. I mean, not really,' Queen paused to draw breath, take a long pull at her cigar and continued.

'You see, he was working on it. Trying it. He thought he could do it. He had the formula. He knew he had got it about right. He had tested it. He said it worked. Not that I ever saw it. I mean, how can you see an invisible man?'

'Pardon?' Pius interjected.

'An invisible man. You know, man you never see. He had done it.'

'Done what, Missis Queen?'

'Made himself invisible. He knew he could do it and he did.'

'Now just a moment.' Pius felt that it was his turn to return some fire before this verbal assault got quite out of hand.

7

'Are you trying to tell me, that your husband, Mister Prince, has disappeared because he has made himself invisible? Because he has done something to himself so that no one can see him? Are you really standing there and telling me that?'

Queen gave Pius another withering look. 'Yes.' she said, 'yes, that's what I am telling you, in short, that is it. He did something to himself and made himself disappear. It has all got to do with his religion. I mean if your religion teaches you that you can control certain vital things then maybe you can. Maybe you can control things which make you disappear. No be so, Mister Shale?' Queen took another long draw at her cigar and puffed a huge cloud of smoke at Pius which slowly enveloped him before being caught up in the draught from the air-conditioner and ultimately dispersed around the room.

It was at this precise point that Pius decided that it would probably be in his best interests and in the general interests of his security service agency if he terminated the conversation and ushered this large and unwholesome lady to the door. However, her next statement made him abruptly change his mind.

'I want you to fly to UK for me.'

Pius looked up at her in amazement. 'Me, fly to UK? But why?'

'To find him.'

'Who?'

'My husband,' the girl bellowed like an angry bush cow. 'My husband, you fool. How was it you ever got a reputation as a secret service agent when your intelligence level is the same as that of a donkey?'

Pius had had enough. He rose from his chair and threw his notebook and pencil on to his desk.

'Missis Queen, I am not sitting here in my own office to be abused by you or by anyone else. I am sorry, but unless you sit down and tell me this story of yours, clearly and intelligently, then I am unable to help you. You are not only wasting my time but also your own by proceeding in this manner. I need a concise explanation before I can begin to offer you any advice whatsoever. Can you give it to me or not?'

Queen hesitated, puffed herself up, pulled at her cigar and blew another cloud of smoke in the general direction of Pius. Then she finally subsided into a chair which creaked and groaned as if in protest.

No wonder Mister Prince has vanished, thought Pius. Who wouldn't want to vanish with this female around!

'OK, Mister Shale, I am sitting and relaxed. I will tell you the whole story and explain to you just why you are going to fly to UK for me and find my Mister Prince.'

Pius had started to protest at her assumption that he was already committed to her cause but she silenced him with a wave of her hand.

'You will work for me,' she said as if in answer to his unspoken protest, 'because I can pay you well and in any currency you name. Now listen...'

For the next thirty minutes Pius sat listening with rapt attention to a story which was so unlikely and bizarre, that when he played back the taped conversation later that day he once again experienced a feeling of total unreality at what was being explained to him. It appeared that Queen's husband,

Mister Prince, was an older man than herself and something of a professional herbalist. Not a man who had learnt traditional medicine in the normal way nor an illiterate possessed of secrets handed down to him from previous generations, but an educated graduate who had decided to study traditional medicine in a thoroughly professional way. According to his wife, at some point in his research Mister Prince had stumbled across a most interesting formula known to our forefathers but long since lost to people to-day. This formula involved not only the drinking of a certain herbal concoction but also a process of thought control which enabled a man to render his body invisible and then to leave it in spirit form. The disbelief which showed on Pius's face when his visitor made this statement quickly vanished under a withering glare of total disdain.

'I am telling you the whole truth and nothing but the truth, Mr Shale, so don't look at me as if I am telling you lies and rubbish.'

Pius membled an apology and Queen went on to explain that at the same time as her husband stumbled on this formula, his life suddenly came under the influence of a religious teacher called Mr Sung. Mr Sung was a Chinaman from Hong Kong who was the head of a religious order called the Milky Wayfarers. Apparently, religion as propounded by Mr Sung hinged on the assertion that each one of us is directly related to a star in the solar system. The millions and millions of stars which make up the Milky Way were, according to Mister Sung, the personal home of every human being on earth – each person having his own individual star. Man, according to this prophet, took a trip through space once every generation and left his personal star behind. Some stars were greater than others and this directly corresponded to a human being's subsequent position on earth in relation to his fellow humans. However, each star had a mother-figure called a Gunk and if a person managed to keep in spiritual touch with his or her Gunk while on earth then a successful earthly life was assured. Mr Sung claimed to have this secret of Gunk contact and Mister Prince, already intoxicated by his discoveries in the world of herbal science, had fallen under the spell of the Milky Wayfarers whose male adherents were represented in this country by one Samson Sigwe.

'But why?' asked Pius at this point summoning up the courage to interrupt the good lady. 'Why should the discovery made by your husband bear any relation to the teaching of this new religion?'

'I am coming to that,' said Queen sharply, clearly ruffled by the interruption. 'I am just coming to that if you can master your obvious impatience, Mr Shale. You see, my husband's main discovery relates to one of the principal pillars of this new religion – the fact that Milky Wayfarers believe that they can escape from their bodies and roam around. What my man has done is to make the physical body disappear after one has left it. In other words, he has enabled a Milky Wayfarer to carry his or her religious doctrine a stage further. Can't you see? The new religion and my man are made for each other. Mister Prince dresses up and chants and dances and has even convinced himself that he is in touch with his own personal Gunk!'

Pius reflected that Queen herself would make a pretty formidable Gunk for any man, but said nothing and let his visitor continue with her story.

'So he has gone off to the convention in UK.'

'Convention?'

'Yes, this Chinaman, Mr Sung, is holding a world-wide convention in UK. As a disciple, Prince was invited along with Samson Sigwe our country's high priest and one or two others. They have all left.'

'OK that's fine', said Pius. 'I can see the story is very, very strange but what is the problem, Missis Queen? Your man has gone to UK to attend an off-beat conference so . . . '

'So he didn't have a ticket', said Queen drily.' The others got a ticket but not my man.'

'And?'

'And he has gone without one. Don't you see, Mr Shale, or must I spell everything out for you? My man Prince said he was not going to get a ticket. He was going to prove to everyone that he was a real Milky Wayfarer. Why, Milky Wayfarers shouldn't have to patronise Sunshine Airways, he said. Catch me buying a ticket. Why, he said, I'll show everyone that I am not talking rubbish. I will just come out of my body, leave for UK and make my body disappear. I will travel free. Do you understand me, Mr Shale?'

'But,' said Pius with a grin which he now found impossible to control, 'what did he propose to do when he got to UK? I mean he couldn't just float around the conference hall, now could he? I mean who would know that he had arrived? Surely, he had to have a body over there to get into when he arrived?'

'That's it, Mr Shale', said Queen, stubbing out her cigar and mashing it into an ashtray. 'That's just it. But he's gone, and his body has gone and he is not booked on any airline and Samson said that he would let my man fly over in his own individual way!' She paused and stared at Pius for fully a minute. It was a stare which seemed to dig deep down into his very soul, and which searched and probed into very private corners of his mind. 'And that is why,' she said in a voice which was as full of menace as a poisoned scorpion's tail, 'that is why you are going to UK, too. You are going to find my man and I have already booked you on the flight which leaves Lagos to-night.'

Chapter Two

It was the advance cash payment which finally persuaded Pius to accept Queen's offer. It was generous and substantial and before he had boarded the internal Sunshine Airways flight to Lagos to catch the late night international flight to UK, he had managed to put it to the credit of the Bisi/Shale Security Agency account. Pius knew just how much their account needed this financial transfusion and therefore Missis Queen's offer had been difficult to refuse.

He had left a brief explanatory note for Bisi who was out on a state government assignment and when he was safely settled on the afternoon flight south, he pulled out of his pocket the typed instructions which Missis Queen had left for him and started to re-read them.

'On no account', he read, 'must my husband come to any harm, Mr Shale. The whole point of your mission is that he must be brought safely back home as quickly as possible. The Milky Wayfarers I find highly distasteful. Mr Sung is probably mad, Mr Sigwe is a crook but Mr Prince, my man, is a genius. The convention is holding on thirteenth July at the Assembly Hall, Pinner, UK. Unless you get my man back, I fear that they will harm him. So, get him back by any means but take care, Mr Sung may be mad but he is highly dangerous. Above all, avoid his eyes. You have been well paid. I trust you will earn your salary.'

Pius re-read the hastily-typed page for the third time and then folded it carefully in his pocket. That is little enough to go on, he thought to himself. If it had not been for the money...

His thoughts were interrupted by the captain's voice which sounded over the plane's intercom. Pius strained to listen as the voice crackled and buzzed overhead. He managed to hear the word Ibadan and so did most of the other passengers on the plane for in an instant everyone seemed to be turning to his neighbour and asking, 'What did he say?' 'What was that?' 'Did you catch that?' Speculation was ended by a handsome stewardess who walked uneasily down the aisle on her high-heeled shoes – non regulation issue.

'We put down for Ibadan,' she said with a frosty stare at each row of passengers in turn, as if daring them to remonstrate with her. 'This plane will not go on to Lagos as scheduled. The fuel is not sufficient to...'

'Fuel? What fuel?' roared an important and pompous-looking, portly gentleman.

'How you never get fuel? You never fill tank?'

'There seems to have been an error of judgement.'

The anger of the passengers was somewhat

softened by fear. Fear that the error of judgement would permit them to get to Ibadan at all! For Pius it was a nuisance but not a disaster. It was only five o'clock, and he estimated that they should be landing at Ibadan at about five-thirty. That would leave plenty of time for him to get a taxi down to Lagos airport and catch the flight to UK which was not due to take-off until half past eleven. But this airline, he thought. Could it really be that someone had forgotten to fill the tank up to the required level?

Exactly one hour and ten minutes later, Pius was speeding down the Ibadan-Lagos Expressway in a brand new yellow and black Toyota taxi whose speedometer registered 6,735 kilometres. The digital watch strapped on to his right wrist was also registering 18-10, and as he looked up out of the window he gave the watch a reassuring pat. It was a recent present from Bisi and one which he valued.

The taxi driver turned up the volume switch on the car radio to such a pitch that the decibels penetrated.

'Hey, cool it,' Pius shouted above the noise, 'I like the music but not the headache.'

The taxi driver whose name had already been established as Jetlag Joe looked at Pius over his shoulder and grinned. 'I get you to de airport before that plane,' he said cheerfully, accelerating to 120 kph.

'The plane ran out of fuel,' replied Pius grimly. 'Don't you run out of or over anything. I value my life. Slow down, Jetlag.'

The driver gave a loud laugh and turned right round to face Pius. 'We all like life, no be so?' he asked.

'You watch the road,' said Pius firmly. 'Otherwise you can stop and let me find another taxi.'

'Or de robber bandits.'

'I know all about the robbers,' said Pius, 'and I would rather take them on single handed than risk my life in your hands at high speed.'

Jetlag Joe laughed again but said nothing and turned back to his driving. It was starting to get dark and Pius had only just managed to notice that the level in the car's petrol tank was getting dangerously low. They would never reach Lagos airport without a refill.

Minutes later, as if in answer to this unspoken thought, Jeglag Joe steered his vehicle wildly off the road and into a large filling station whose forecourt was covered in oil which appeared to have seeped from a disabled and battered tanker. They skidded on the oil patch and the taxi slewed to a halt.

'These dirty people. Roads in Nigeria are good,' Jetlag Joe shouted to nobody in particular out of the window. 'They good for killing people.'

He manouvered the taxi towards a petrol pump and an attendant sauntered over to fill it up. He was a nondescript individual with deep scarification which together with smallpox scars and the results of an accident to the right hand side of his face, made his appearance memorable to say the least. The man said nothing as he accepted payment for the petrol but for a moment subjected Pius to a long and searching look.

'Come on, come on, he go to Ikeja airport.' Jetlag Joe called out. 'He no get time to wait for you to move yourself.'

The man leered at Pius for a moment and

whispered, 'You go for UK?'

'What's it to you?'

'Have a good ride.' The attendant slammed shut the car door and Jetlag switched on the ignition. The engine spluttered for a moment and then burst into life. They drove rapidly through the oily patch and out on to the Expressway. As they started to draw away from the petrol station, Pius suddenly noticed another car pulling out behind them. It was a smart, green Mercedes and Pius was certain that it had not been on the forecourt when they had filled up. He frowned for a moment and then addressed himself to Jetlag Joe who had started to drive as though he was about to enter the Sokoto car rally.

'I tell you, you go slow,' shouted Pius. 'What for you race like this?'

'Robbers,' shouted Joe back at him. 'Robbers. I no like this road after dark and we still get long way to go.'

Pius sat back in his seat. He knew it was going to be one of those do or die rides with little attention being paid to him or to his safety. He tried to concentrate his mind on other things as Jetlag turned up the volume switch on the car radio.

They overtook a lumbering mammy wagon whose painted slogan ALL ROAD GO TO GOD seemed a little too apt for Pius's peace of mind.

He forced himself to think about the strange interview he had had with Queen, about the Milky Wayfarers and their Gunks, and started to wonder why on earth he had bothered to get mixed up in this crazy adventure.

At that moment the green Mercedes came up behind them. They must have been travelling at at least 130 kph, when with lights flashing and horn blaring it suddenly appeared on their tail. Jetlag Joe swung the taxi violently to the left and made a rude gesture with his hand as the Mercedes flashed past him. However, this reckless action appeared to make Jetlag want to travel even faster, and in spite of the Mercedes more powerful engine they were soon driving on its tail. Then Pius saw the gun. A side window had been lowered at the back of the Mercedes and a figure was leaning out of it with a high velocity rifle fitted with a telescopic sight. It was trained on Pius. Instinctively he ducked and as he did so he grabbed Jetlag's hair and pulled him sharply out of his seat like a human shield. There was a crack, a smash of glass and a sharp cry from Jetlag as the Toyota spun away from the right hand track at a terrifying speed. Pius scrambled into the vacant driver's seat and grabbed the steering column. The car was heading straight for the crash barrier at the side of the road and he knew that if they hit it at this speed, they would somersault into the bush and he would inevitably be killed outright.

He pulled the wheel round and the hubs of the nearside rear wheel scraped the barrier. The car rocketed back towards the centre of the road just missing a Volkswagen bus as it did so.

Pius knew that if he straightened the wheel abruptly they would spin right round in the middle of the road and end up facing the oncoming traffic which would result in an equally hideous accident. He pulled the wheel round once more but this time pulled too sharply and the car spun round a full 180 degrees before continuing on an erratic course back towards the far side of the road. He suddenly spotted

19

a gap in the barrier just ahead of him where another driver had met an inglorious end. He just managed to steer the car through it and on to a muddy bank by the side of the road, narrowly avoiding a large hole which had been excavated for laterite.

He glanced at Jetlag Joe. A 25 millimetre hole had been neatly drilled in the centre of his forehead by a bullet which had undoubtedly been meant for Pius himself. He smiled grimly, opened the passenger door and pushed Jetlag Joe through it and on to the ground outside. He glanced up to see whether he could see the green Mercedes but it had vanished so he slammed the door shut and reversed the taxi back on to the road. No one had stopped, no one had bothered to take the slightest interest in his predicament. As far as the other road drivers were concerned, it was the survival of the fittest on that particular stretch of the road and 'Love thy Neighbour' played no part whatsoever in their philosophy.

I expect that the garage attendant was in league with them, mused Pius, and tipped them off when we filled up at the station. There is no doubt that they were trying to record a direct hit on the taxi's passenger! Pius also knew that Jetlag Joe would be left to lie there until bloated by the sun and covered with flies he was either taken by a predator or the police. Most likely the former.

No mercy on the Expressway, he thought, as he raced through ninety and up to a hundred kph, trying to spot the rear light of a Mercedes in front of him. Not that traffic was heavy, few people wished to chance the Expressway after dark. All at once he saw it. He had just passed another filling station when he noticed the green Mercedes parked by the entrance with its nose towards the road. No doubt waiting for my dead driver to pull in and share the loot, he thought. The Mercedes driver spotted him as he sped by and realising that something had gone wrong, began to give chase once more. Its superior speed soon had it hugging the Toyota's tail. Pius thought rapidly. Unless I move fast they will have me with that high velocity rifle, he thought. Then he remembered an old trick, taught to him when he had visited Zaire three years previously. He put his foot down as hard as he could, at the same time hugging the central crash barrier until the hub caps of his off-side wheels were practically touching the heavy metal girder. Although the Mercedes was still on his tail, it was not quite as close to the barrier as the Toyota. In fact, it was lying nearly three quarters the width of a car away from it. He gritted his teeth and abruptly applied the brakes. The driver behind him was left with only one choice. He had to pull to the left or he would either hit Pius or the central barrier. He pulled to the left and Pius pressed hard on the accelerator causing the Toyota to virtually leap into the air. As he did so, he heard the satisfying sound of a crash followed immediately by the rending of metal and the smashing of glass. The Mercedes had crashed out of control into the far roadside barrier just as he had hoped it would. For the time being he was safe and he whispered a prayer of gratitude to Ferdinand Otu who had, by his simple strategy, saved his life.

The excitement and tension of the past three minutes had been sufficient for half a life time and Pius found that he was not only drenched in sweat but shaking violently as well. He mopped his brow with a yellow duster and sped on towards Lagos and the airport.

The rest of the journey was totally without incident until he reached Ikeja. There he encountered a monumental go-slow and although he had time in hand he hadn't imagined spending it stuck in a car without the ability to go either forward or back. He cursed and mopped his brow. Pedlars and hawkers were swarming around the stationary cars like bees around a hive trying to sell every imaginable range of stolen or smuggled goods from whisky to miniature television sets.

'Look, look! Buy dis one!'

'You see him! He fine, fine one! Only ten naira!'

'Look, man, look!'

Pius made sure the car doors were secure and the windows tightly sealed. He switched on the radio and leant back in his seat, trying his best to ignore the grinning faces at the car windows and the entreaties made by the thugs and layabouts.

Suddenly he heard a banging sound from behind. It was immediately clear what was happening. Someone was trying to open the car boot and to remove his luggage from out of it. He congratulated himself mentally that he had insisted that his hold-all was put inside with him, in spite of the protestations of Jetlag Joe at the time. Nevertheless, he watched in utter helplessness as the thieves prised open the boot, proceeded to take out the spare wheel and the jack, and walked off with them proudly displayed on their heads for all the world to see. Piu knew full well that in his own interest it would be better to sit tight where he was, for if he got out and exposed himself to the mob of hawkers outside, he would be in grave danger of losing not only his suitcase, but all his clothing as well!

The other drivers behind and on either side of him deliberately remained completely aloof from what was going on. They did not want to attract unwanted attention to their own luggage, and they certainly did not want to appear at any court proceedings as a witness to theft. 'Hear no evil, see no evil,' was their very strict motto.

At last the traffic began to move slowly forward and the leering, grinning faces of the hawkers were slowly removed from the windows of the taxi, where the steam from their breath left grotesque patterns resembling the death masks of corpses.

Three minutes later a bumping sound from the rear off-side wheel indicated to Pius beyond any shadow of doubt that he had a puncture. He glanced briefly at his mirror and saw to his horror that a group of thugs were jogging along the pavement beside him. The obscene grins on their faces told him all he needed to know. Having stolen his spare wheel, they had now succeeded in puncturing his tyre. Clearly, they were determined to pick up his hold-all on the back seat. Already the group had pushed in front of the car directly behind him, waiting to push him off the road when he finally brought the car to a halt. This was something which Pius was determined not to do. Punctured tyre or not, he knew that at all costs he must keep driving. The traffic was moving faster now and he pushed his foot hard on the accelerator at first to the amusement and then to the obvious dismay of the group of thugs behind him.

23

Chapter Three

When Pius Shale reached the airport car park the car's rear axle and the rear wheel hub were so badly bent that they would need completely replacing before the car could ever be taken on the road again. A new crowd of touts and layabouts had been attracted by the entrance of the crippled taxi and had immediately surrounded it on its arrival. They seemed very angry.

'Hey, you there. Mr Taximan,' one burly, pock-marked individual shouted at Pius. 'What for you drive that thing so he go spoil?'

'You fool man,' another thug shouted at him. 'You go spoil that your car.'

'That no be his car,' shouted yet another man who had pushed his way to the front of the crowd. 'That car be for na Ibadan man. I know de man tho' I no know de name. How you get this car?' he shouted rudely at Pius.

But the last thing Pius was going to do was to get involved in a senseless argument with a group of idle layabouts. He was determined to get into the airport building as quickly as possible together with his small hold-all which contained not only his clothes but also the papers and instructions both for the flight and for the investigation which he had undertaken on behalf of Queen. He clipped a handcuff which he had taken out of his jacket pocket on to the handle of the hold-all and then fastened the other end to his right wrist. If they were going to take his bag then they would have to take his arm as well, he thought grimly. He eased himself into the front passenger seat to give the crowd the impression that he was about to make an exit from the left-hand side of the car. Immediately the mob crowded round that side. Then he made his move. In a flash he returned to the driver's seat, opened the door and jumped out into the car park. One tough looking boy tried to grab his hold-all but he swung the case neatly out of his grasp and sprinted towards the airport building.

'Stop, tief man, stop.' They were shouting at him now and several bona-fide passengers gave him curious looks as he dived into a crowd which had gathered in a confused and disorderly group outside the building.

'Hey, Mr Man, who do you think you are?'

'Why you be so anxious. Cool yourself, man.'

Pius ignored the protesting voices and pushed his way towards the long struggling mass of exasperated humanity which formed the queue to get on flight 800, the flight to London, UK.

Immediately he reached the queue which had deteriorated into a mass of shouting perspiring and exasperated fellow-countrymen he knew that something was wrong. The actions of a large, fat

25

man dressed in an impeccable, blue, pin-striped suit told him all he wanted to know. He was waving his yellow ticket over the head of an equally large and exasperated female whose elaborate head-tie had come undone and was trailing on the ground behind her.

'You can't overbook me. I get ticket since, since, since,' the man was shouting. 'How dare you overbook me and my wife! How dare you. I will report this.'

Pius groaned inwardly. The overbooking was clearly not confined to a few passengers. At least six had been ordered to the back of the queue while the position was being regularised.

A harassed airport official started to plead with the fat and important-looking gentleman and then with his wife. When this appeared to have no effect he started to shout at him.

'We tell you to wait,' he said. 'You are not on the flight list. I don't care whether you booked this morning or a year ago, your name is not on the tele-printer so you must wait.'

'But I paid . . .'

'I no care what you pay. Just because you pay it never mean you get seat! Don't you know that?' The official imparted this piece of unanswerable logic as if it was the most obvious statement in the world. After all, payment was only half the battle. Obtaining a vacant seat was the much more important other half and the more difficult.

'But I tell you,' the woman shouted, 'there is no other airline in the world . . .'

'I know that,' said the official, screaming at the top of his voice. 'But this is Nigeria! You understand

26

me, this is Nigeria!'

He was suddenly swept off his feet as the shouting, gesticulating mob of passengers swept forward. A family of six who had been at the front of the queue and who had managed to obtain seats left in a rush for the custom area and the crowd swarmed to fill the vacuum.

The airport official disappeared in the crush and Pius was lifted bodily off his feet and propelled forward. As this happened, a sharp jerk of his right arm told him that someone had attempted to snatch his firmly secured hold-all. He glanced quickly to his right but whoever it was had immediately been swallowed up in the swirl of sweating humanity.

'Hey, na me. I get ticket.'

'Look! look! Hey, my friend. Look for this one.'

A baby started to scream. An elderly gentleman had his spectacles knocked off his nose and smashed underfoot. Chaos reigned.

Then the officials who were trying to cope with the impossible task of sorting out the overbooking problem did the obvious thing. They walked away from behind their heavily protected grille.

'We no work til you people line up,' an official shouted as he walked through a door into an office behind him.

The fury of the passengers increased. Confronted as they were with no one to deal with them, unable even to speak to someone who would ensure that they would get a seat, they raised their voices to their Lord and Maker.

'Oh, my good God.' a man shouted. 'Help us. Save this our country.'

As if in answer to this heartfelt prayer, a group of

soldiers who had been standing in one corner of the airport suddenly took it upon themselves to remedy a situation which was rapidly turning into a small-scale riot.

Without the benefit of an officer to restrain them, they cocked their rifles and advanced towards the group of enraged passengers. As they reached the battling mob one of them raised his rifle butt and brought it savagely down on the head of the large, fat man whose protestation against overbooking, in spite of advance payment, had been the root cause of the whole incident. Blood suddenly streamed down his face and without a murmur he sank to the floor.

His wife who had by this time not only lost her head-dress but her wrapper as well, started to scream in Yoruba until another savage blow on her buttocks sent her reeling into the mob.

Two other soldiers aimed at the mob with their rifles in a singularly ominous fashion.

'Don't you point dis thing at me,' said another large middle-aged Yoruba dressed in a colourful *agbada*. As if in answer, the soldier concerned jabbed his rifle end sharply into the pit of the man's stomach and he too sank to the floor groaning and sobbing in agony.

By this time, the mob had got the message. Unless the situation was brought speedily under control, these four soldiers were clearly going to take someone's life and that was a much more important matter than getting a seat on flight 800.

A hush fell on the hall broken only by the sobs of the prostrate man and woman. The passengers shuffled into a line and by some strange twist of fate Pius found himself manoeuvered into the very front of the queue. As an officer appeared and started giving wild orders to his soldiers, the two officials who had been originally dealing with the tickets re-appeared from the office behind the grille.

'You, what's your name?'

'Pius Shale.'

The official looked down at his flight manifest.

'How do you spell, Shale?'

'S.H.A.L.E.'

Pius gave a huge sigh of relief as the official spotted his name. Queen had clearly known how to make a booking.

'Smoking?'

'Non-smoking, please.'

'Luggage?'

'Hand luggage.'

'Let's see.'

Pius held up his hold-all.

'OK. Next.'

Pius could not believe his luck. He hastily left the scene of confusion and bloodshed behind him and putting his boarding card into his shirt pocket, made for the passport control area. All proceeded smoothly until he arrived at the currency check counter. The official in charge eyed him suspiciously.

'Where's the form?'

Pius handed him the currency form which revealed that he was taking out traveller's cheques to a value of £500. Queen had made suitable arrangements should this prove inadequate.

'You get naira?'

'No, naira except for three,' said Pius perfectly honestly.

The man gave him a cold glare. 'Why you chain the bag to your wrist?'

'I guess you would if you could see what's going on out there,' said Pius giving a sharp nod towards the booking hall.

'Let me see in.'

Pius unlocked the handcuffs and then the hold-all. He knew that this official would never discover the false bottom which had so cleverly been stitched into it by his Italian friend Dario. It had never been discovered yet, and he had used it this time to conceal the sparse information and instructions which Queen had given to him.

The official rumaged through Pius's few personal belongings. He undid the wash bag and picked up his expensive electric razor.

'Where you get this?'

Pius answered the question by asking another.

'Aren't you supposed to be dealing with currency? The customs man is over there.'

'Where you get this,' the man persisted, eyeing the razor in obvious admiration.

'In Tokyo,' said Pius truthfully.

'Show me visa for Tokyo.'

Now although Pius had indeed bought the razor in Tokyo, his mission to Japan had been so delicate and confidential and essential to the Nigerian authorities that he had slipped in under diplomatic cover. No passport had been needed in that particular instance and he was fully aware that this official, who was conspicuously exceeding his authority, would not find a Japanese stamp. Nevertheless, Pius handed him his passport.

A small queue had by this time started to form

behind Pius composed of other passengers who had been lucky enough to find that they were booked on the flight. Their murmurings at further delay started to turn once again to shouts of protest.

'Hey, come on. We have to catch a plane.'

'Let us through please, Mr Official.'

The official glanced at the passengers to assess their importance. In his view a few merited attention, so he turned to Pius and said, 'Wait.'

'What do you mean, wait?' protested Pius. 'My currency is in order. What do you mean, wait? It's because he is interested in my razor,' he said turning to the important-looking gentleman in the queue behind him.

'Your razor is no concern of mine,' said the man pushing himself forward and at the same time elbowing Pius out of the way. 'Here, Mr Official, take my currency form.'

Pius stood to one side. He knew that his special agent's card could have got him past this hurdle with comparative ease, but it was something he was very reluctant to use in front of strangers, especially when he was on a job.

He stood to one side and the official whose mind was now quite clearly concentrated on obtaining the electric razor for himself, took the currency forms of the assembled passengers without questioning one of them. When the last man had gone he turned to Pius.

'I never see the stamp for Tokyo in your book.'

'Try Japan,' said Pius.

'I never see that either.'

Pius was tempted to make a sarcastic remark about the need for spectacles but as the stamp was clearly not in his passport he thought better of it.

'So?'

'I take the razor,' said the official firmly.

'No, my friend,' said Pius sharply. 'I have taken your number it is stored here,' he tapped his head. 'and I will make sure the head of your service gets to know about your secondary occupation which seems to me to have no connection with checking currency certificates.'

The official laughed. 'You tell my boss and he will take the razor for himself!'

Pius looked up at him in exasperation. 'You mean you will steal it.'

'No I will confiscate it,' the official paused, '... legally.'

'Legally?'

'Yes, legally. You say you buy him for Tokyo. Yet there is no record of you visiting Tokyo. Therefore putting two together with two to make four I assume you require it by illegal currency methods.'

'What!'

'You get receipt?'

'No.'

'Why not?'

'Because I buy him in Tokyo two years ago. I grow beard every day. I cut beard every day. I need razor. I no need receipt.'

Another crowd of passengers had gathered behind Pius. The previous scene was about to be re-enacted and the official was on the point of asking Pius to stand aside once more. He was determined to have the razor. Pius who was still as determined not to reveal his identity decided to take the easy way out. He snapped his hold-all shut and said quietly,

32

'OK, keep it,' and walked rapidly away.

Pius was inwardly seething at the way in which the corrupt official had got away with such a blatant theft of his property, but he knew from long experience that an agent's identity had to remain secret, especially when confronted with unknown officialdom. It was one of the hard lessons which someone in his profession had to learn. 'Discretion and no scene,' as Bisi had once succinctly-put it.

His attention was diverted by another official this time in the form of a customs officer who called out to him as he walked up the customs area deep in thought.

'Hey you! Why you no let us check the bag? You think you walk straight on the plane without a check?'

'I am sorry,' said Pius discreetly obeying the second golden rule: never pick a quarrel with an official.

'I see you are in a hurry, my friend,' said the customs officer somewhat mollified by Pius's subservient attitude. 'Maybe you get something you want to hide.'

'Not at all,' said Pius. 'I was thinking and didn't see you.'

'You been to currency?' enquired the official.

'Yes, currency check me.'

'Where is the form?'

'What . . . ?' Pius stared at the man in disbelief. In his haste to get away from the official thief on the currency desk he had forgotten to take back his currency form. He ran back to the man who motioned him to go to the back of the queue. Twenty minutes later with take-off time having moved significantly closer he was back with the customs official.

'You get the form now?'

'Yes.'

'Good, let me see your bag.'

Once again, rough hands rummaged through the sparse contents.

'I see you never carry razor,' said the official eventually as he scribbled with a piece of pink chalk on the side of the hold-all.

'No,' said Pius, 'but if you ever need a quick shave just go and see your colleague in currency. I am sure that he has got just the thing.'

Chapter Four

'Sunshine Airways regret to announce the delay in departure to flight 800 to Kano and London. This is on account of technical difficulties. We request passengers to remain in the departure area and listen for further announcements.' Pius Shale groaned. He knew that this could mean anything from a one to ten hour delay. Man proposes, God and Sunshine Airways disposes, he thought grimly to himself. And there is still the ordeal of the final security check as well . . .'

He cocked an eye at the soberly-dressed individual who had come out of the VIP lounge for the third time and who was looking about him in a somewhat agitated fashion. Pius hadn't noticed him in the crush to get on to the plane but since his arrival in the departure lounge the man had caught his attention. He really does seem most concerned about something, he mused to himself as the man disappeared rapidly behind the green door marked VIP in large, white letters.

Not for the first time that day, Pius thought about the strange mission which he had undertaken and the more he thought about it the stranger it seemed. How could he begin to look for a man who claimed to have left his body? What should he begin to look for when both had disappeared, the body or the man?

A thick-set, soldierly-looking man had walked briskly into the departure lounge and stopped beside the bench where Pius was sitting. He looked sharply round about him. He glanced anxiously at his watch and Pius ran a carefully trained eye up from his highly-polished shoes to his nearly-white shirt collar. From his bright expensive tie to the chunky ring on his carefully manicured finger.

Ibo, possibly a soldier, possibly a former soldier turned businessman. Officer class, he thought to himself. Successful but anxious. Money but problems. He indexed the dapper, little man and stored him in the filing cabinet of his mind.

'Excuse me, has there been a delay?' The man was looking down at Pius with an impatient and penetrating stare.

'Yes, there sure has,' said Pius. 'Technical hitch and no new timetable for take-off.'

'How disgraceful,' said the man. 'Really this airline is too bad.'

Pius ignored the invitation to discuss the merits or otherwise of Sunshine Airways and opted to dig further. Just for interest's sake as it were.

'You going to UK?'

'Yes,' the man replied, giving Pius a swift glance as though checking on his credentials. 'Yes, I am.'

'Business?'

'Of a sort. How about you?'

'Yes,' said Pius deciding to use his carefully rehearsed cover story, 'I am in the drug trade.'

The man's eyes flickered for an instant. 'Really, and how are drugs these days?'

'Everything is difficult these days. I am sure you know the problems. Currency hold-ups, M forms, restrictions, delays, smuggling. I expect you know it all as well as I do.'

The stranger nodded and glanced quickly about him. Pius had remained seated and so was able to read the initials 'S.S.' on the man's brief-case as he waved it impatiently in front of him.

'What sort of drugs?' asked the man disinterestedly. 'Ordinary Kingsway Chemist-type drugs?'

Pius decided to have a gamble on this Ibo gentleman – after all there was just a chance...

'No, herbal.'

The man's interest in Pius quickened noticibly. The reply had caught his attention and Pius knew at once that quite unexpectedly, his shaft had struck home.

'How very interesting,' said the man. 'How most interesting.' He sat down on the bench beside Pius and stared hard into his face.

'So you are a herbalist?'

'Of a sort.'

'You don't look that kind of man to me.'

'Perhaps not,' said Pius, resolving to let this bizarre conversation run on, 'but looks are not everything you know.'

'Yes, I do know,' said the other man with heavy emphasis on the 'do'. 'I do know indeed, but it is

37

strange, to say the least, to find a modern, young man like you interested in such an old-fashioned thing.'

'Maybe it is, but I am sure you know that a good deal of what used to be considered old-fashioned rubbish and was suppressed by the colonialists as tribal and bush, is now being considered in a new light,' said Pius with great enthusiasm.

'Really?'

'Yes, and if I may say so, as you are not so old yourself, your obvious interest in the subject proves the point.'

'I am interested from a religious aspect,' said the man and as he said it Pius knew that chance had indeed provided him with a meeting with Samson Sigwe, who no doubt was travelling to UK to attend the Milky Wayfarers convention. He played his ace card.

'That is interesting because my uncle, Mr Prince, is . . .'

Samson Sigwe, for it was indeed he, was staring at Pius in utter astonishment and he suddenly interrupted him.

'You mean, Mr Prince, husband of Missis Queen – is she your aunt?'

'You know them?' asked Pius innocently.

Mr Sigwe's eyes narrowed for a moment as if he was deciding on his next line of approach. All at once he had become very interested in Pius Shale and the fact that their flight had been delayed had completely vanished from his mind.

'Yes, I know your uncle well. In fact we belong to the same religion.'

'I had heard he was mixed up in some new sect,'

said Pius. 'Milkers or some juju like that?

Samson Sigwe ignored the comment and hurried on to his next question. 'Did your uncle train you?'

'Of course – he is a leading authority in herbalism.'

'And are you acquainted with his discoveries?'

Pius paused and then looking Samson fully in the face said quite softly, 'Yes, nearly all of them.'

For a moment Samson Sigwe seemed stunned, then he recovered himself.

'I believe your uncle had made a very important discovery concerning spirit travel – are you aware of that?'

'Intimately.'

At that moment, the gentleman who had been appearing and reappearing from out of the VIP lounge suddenly emerged, spotted Samson and with a delighted grin 'of recognition on his face, strode over towards him with arm outstretched.

'Samson – I have been looking all over for you. I thought maybe you had been double-booked like those poor unfortunates out there. And now we have this terrible wait.'

'Ah, Luka,' said Samson taking his eyes reluctantly from Pius. 'I was held up for a time but here I am. Luka, I want to introduce you to a most interesting person. No less than our brother, Mr Prince's nephew, Mr . , . '

'Mr Prince Junior. Julius Prince,' said Pius quickly.

'How very, very interesting,' said the stranger with an intensity matched only by that of Samson himself. 'How extremely interesting. Are you one of us?'

'If you mean am I a member of my uncle's sect the answer is no,' said Pius. 'I am just a good orthodox Roman Catholic.'

The two men exchanged glances.

'Mr Prince Junior is a herbalist. Well versed in his uncle's secrets. Isn't that right, Julius?'

'Yes, that's what I told you,' said Pius with a smile although instinctively he was beginning to form an unfavourable impression of Mr Sigwe and his friend.

'And he is off to UK to buy new stock for importation into our country.'

'That's right. Are you two gentlemen going on business to UK?'

'No, we are off to our convention. It's a world-wide affair and is held annually on a rotational basis in a different country. This time it is the UK's turn.'

'Will my uncle be there?'

Samson smiled, 'We hope so. We certainly hope so. Luka,' he said turning to his companion, 'I think our friend here should sit next to me on the journey. I would very much like to talk to him if and when we take off. Do you think you would be kind enough to exchange boarding passes with him?'

'Of course, Samson,' said Luka promptly. 'I am sure you will learn much from each other.'

'Sunshine Airways announce that the technical problem for flight 800 from Lagos to Kano and London is now under control. Will passengers please collect all their hand luggage and proceed to security check.'

'Not as long a technical hitch as we feared,' said Samson with a smile. 'Come, Julius, let us proceed.'

Pius's mind was working overtime. He knew that it would be impossible to keep up the pretence of being Prince's nephew if he was subjected to intense questioning by Sigwe. However, as luck has thrown them together, it would be unwise not to take advantage of their meeting. After all, he was on a paid job...

He decided to let the two men go ahead of him into security. It was better if they were out of the way when he went through, for if security became troublesome he would be forced to use his identity card.

'Excuse me while I go to the toilet,' he said to Samson as they got up from the travel-stained bench. I'll see you in the final departure lounge.'

Without waiting for a reply he walked quickly towards the toilets. Once inside a vacant cubicle he removed the handcuffs from his pocket and placed them behind the water cistern. When he returned to the main departure lounge, Samson and Luka had already disappeared through the door.

He hung back for five minutes and then went through the door himself.

There were two men and a woman searching the hand luggage of the passengers. Another man was frisking their clothing before they finally left the security area. Pius waited his turn and then walked over to the counter. As he did so, the girl came over to him and said in a clear voice, 'Open the bag, please!' It was Bisi.

Pius fumbled with his lock stalling for time. Bisi had clearly gone to a great deal of trouble to make sure that she was on the security check when he passed through.

'Open the bag, please.' said Bisi with lowered eye-lids.

Pius opened his hold-all and Bisi rummaged through it. As she did so, Pius noticed her drop a folded piece of paper on to a crumpled shirt.

'OK,' she said smartly. 'Next.'

For an instant their eyes met and Bisi momentarily narrowed hers and jerked them upwards, indicating to Pius that he should pocket the paper before shutting the case. This he did, moved on to a man who ran his hands clumsily over his body in an inadequate search for a weapon, and then made for the final departure area.

Samson Sigwe and Luka were standing waiting to welcome him as he passed through the door. Samson seemed unnaturally friendly.

'Ah, Julius,' he shouted. 'No problem I trust!'

'Not at all, not at all. They are not concerned with innocents like me.'

Samson laughed. 'Of course not. Come and join us, we have a seat over here.'

Pius who was desperately anxious to read the message from Bisi was unable to do anything further for his arm was firmly grasped and he was led over to a free place on a bench which Samson and Luka had reserved with their hand luggage.

'Now then, sit down...'

'Sunshine Airways announce the departure of flight 800 to Kano and London. Will passengers please extinguish their cigarettes and proceed with their hand luggage to the bus which will take them to the aircraft.'

'That's us' said Samson with a nod to Luka and Pius.

'Come along, Julius, it may be overbooked.'

Pius, exasperated at still being unable to read

Bisi's message which he knew must be urgent, was pushed forward towards the exit doors by a crowd of passengers carrying every conceivable kind of hand luggage. Once outside, he was suddenly stopped from getting into the waiting bus by Samson who took a strong grip on his arm.

'I am sure that the plane is overbooked,' he said. 'Don't take the bus. Let's run for the plane and get first in the queue.'

A group of other passengers overheard the remark and began to shout out to those behind them.

Overbook. Overbook. Run for the plane.'

Immediately chaos ensued. Passengers who were on the bus tried to get off. The driver tried to close the doors only to find that he had trapped a mother who had a baby strapped to her back. The child screamed. The mother yelled. The driver swore.

Meanwhile a surging tide of passengers raced towards the waiting plane.

'Overbook! Overbook! Run! Run!'

An air hostess who was at the bottom of the aircraft's steps waiting to collect boarding passes, looked in horror at the howling mob who was rushing towards her.

'They go kill me,' she muttered and ran away to the other side of the plane despite the protestations of a lone security guard. However, as the screaming passengers drew closer, he, too, took to his heels.

'Overbook! Overbook!'

The cry turned from one of panic to one of menace.

Pius, Luka and Samson were carried forward by

the momentum of the mob. Unable to resist or slow down, they ran for their lives.

The narrow gangway drew closer. The first two or three passengers managed to leap up the steps and into the plane. Another air hostess stood shouting at the top of the steps. 'Stop, all of you, stop. You must wait for check.' But when she saw the mood of the angry mob she fled to the safety of the plane's toilet and bolted the door.

The main body of the mob converged on the steps and immediately there was a jam. Women screamed, men cursed. One man who had no boarding card smartly flicked a card out of another man's coat pocket.

A woman started howling, 'My leg! My leg! You have broken my leg!'

Unheeding, unyielding the mob shoved and pushed until finally the surging mass of gesticulating, sweating humanity was squeezed up the steps like sausage meat being forced into a skin.

Pius was flung tightly against Samson, so tightly that he felt every ripple of his muscular body as they were squeezed forward. Even in the utter confusion, his brain told him that the man was strong and very, very tough. As he reached the entrance door to the plane, his jacket caught on a catch and it tore as he pulled it away. His boarding card disappeared but somehow he managed to keep a grip on his hold-all. He was luckier than other passengers. Some luggage was trampled underfoot. One or two cases were snatched away from the unwary by the unscrupulous.

Once in the plane, it soon became clear that every single member of the crew and cabin staff had fled and secured themselves safely behind bolted doors.

Samson pulled Pius into a seat beside him. 'Don't move,' he shouted. 'We have made it.'

Luka dived into a seat directly behind them. There were more screams as a child was separated from its mother. The mother tried to withstand the forward surge of the passengers in order to make her way back to her child but in the process was thrown bodily on top of another passenger who was already seated.

'Get off me you...'

'My baby. They will kill my baby.'

Pius closed his eyes. The noise, screams and general confusion made it difficult to think. Yet think he must.

'This is my seat.'

'No, I dey get him.'

'Get off this plane.'

More shouts, more confusion. Suddenly, as if a gushing tap had been abruptly switched off, the pushing and shoving stopped. The last few passengers were able to walk calmly through the aircraft door. There had been no overbooking, there was a seat for everyone and even one or two spare. The screaming woman whose leg had indeed been broken, was carried away by her husband.

'I will sue you all,' he shouted hysterically. 'Every damn one of you. And this my airline. And this my country. I will sue you all. Damn you all.' The man made a defiant gesture with his lips and left the plane. The child was reunited with its mother. The passengers checked their baggage and licked their wounds. One by one, the cabin crew emerged from their hiding-places.

One tall air hostess, whose wig had been knocked to the side of her head, and whose make-up was smudged and tear-stained stood up in the middle of the aisle.

'What for you behave like that?' she shouted. 'Who do you think you people are?'

Some of the passengers had already started to relax.

'Get the plane into the air,' a large important-looking business man shouted.

'Stop your lecture and get on with it.'

'Get the pilot in action.'

'I must see your boarding-passes,' the girl screamed back at them. 'I must see each one of your passes.'

'Oh, go away. Don't you know half of us lost them in that rush?'

'I must see...'

But the girl's protests were drowned by the passengers who with one voice roared at her to shut up. They had had enough.

Suddenly there was a crackle and a voice sounded over the plane's loudspeakers.

'Hallo, this is your flight steward, Victor Awoniyi, speaking. We are shortly due to take-off and you are asked to fasten...'

The voice droned on giving the standard safety instructions as if nothing untoward had happened. The passengers relaxed. The angry hostess retreated.

'Here, try some of this,' said Samson handing Pius a half bottle of whisky. 'I guess you need it.'

Pius hesitated, it wasn't his normal practice to drink at this time, but then this trip so far had been not at all normal. He didn't like Samson Sigwe, he had a note he must somehow read. He . . .

'Thanks.' Pius took a long pull at the bottle. The whisky slipped down his throat, burning as it went. Somehow he felt that it was not like any whisky he had ever taken before. He shook his head and glanced at Samson who seemed to be looking at Pius with a curious smile on his face. Pius blinked and shook his head again. Things seemed to be revolving round about him. The plane seemed to be turning upside down. Samson Sigwe had two heads. No he had three, now four.

He let out a faint cry of protest and slumped forward in his seat.

Chapter Five

'Is everything ready for the opening session?' asked
Mr Sung. 'Is everything in order at the hall?'

The young Nigerian who was asked the question
nodded his head vigorously for a moment and then
said, 'Yes, our Father, everything is ready.'

Mr Sung smiled at the youth and clapped his
chubby hands together three times. 'Good, good. I
am pleased with you, Victor. Your organising ability
is very pleasing to me. You will go far in our
movement.'

'Thank you, our Father.'

Mr Sung was always addressed as 'our Father'. It
was a custom he had initiated when he first gathered
the seven disciples around him twelve years
previously and founded the Milky Wayfarers. Even
now, although the religion had grown to its present
size of over a thousand adherents throughout the
world, he was always addressed in the same
reverential manner. He was a small man, plump, but
not grossly fat, with a face which was curiously

wizened like a little, old man. He could not be more than fifty, but years of prayer and contemplation had not stamped his face with the mark of serenity, but rather had left him with worry lines and wrinkles which criss-crossed his oriental features like an unevenly constructed spider's web. He wore a brightly-coloured robe, embroidered in silk with snakes and fiery dragons. The predominant colour of this garment was bright yellow and he had never been seen dressed in anything else. He had a wardrobe of over twenty embroidered and elaborate yellow robes of the identical pattern.

The particular yellow which he used highlighted the most curious aspect of him, his eyes. These, besides being singularly compelling when he spoke either to an individual or to a mass sycophantic audience, were coloured bright green.

Even during his early years in the poverty stricken slums of Hong Kong, his remarkable eyes had enabled him to dominate his contemporaries and convince his destitute parents that they had brought a special being into the world. Mr Sung had quickly realised that he could use this special gift to powerful effect. At the age of eight he had a vision. When he was sixteen he received a message; by the age of twenty-two he had a complete revelation from outer space. On the strength of that he had founded his religion – the Milky Wayfarers.

His seven original disciples, friends from his earliest youth, had taken his message far and wide. At first they and Mr Sung were abused and treated to ridicule. But gradually the followers and believers increased until the tide of scepticism turned and people from foreign lands and of different beliefs

49

foresook their traditions and turned to Mr Sung and the Milky Wayfarers for inspiration and guidance. They were young, mostly under thirty, and by convincing them that their Gunk was always approachable, always contactable, always ready to advance their prospects on earth, Mr Sung managed to attract youth who had been disaffected and disillusioned. He inspired them to follow a code where there was hope, not only for a future after death, but for prosperity on this earth.

And he had success. Fired with a new enthusiasm, the poor, or certain well-publicised individual members of the poor, received wealth and success as followers of Mr Sung. One of the principle reasons they were able to do this according to the adherents of this new cult, was on account of their ability to 'spirit roam' at will. To leave their bodies and move about all-knowing yet unseen in exactly the same way as Mr Prince claimed to be able to do.

Victor smiled at his leader, but turned hastily away from the penetrating green eyes for Mr Sung was not just revered by his followers but also greatly feared.

'Shall I leave you, our Father? Do you wish to have quiet before the opening session?'

'Sit down, Victor, on the floor over there. Sit down a moment there is something I want to say to you.'

Victor sat down. Orphaned from birth he had been 'saved' by Mr Sung in Lagos from a life of brutality and crime and had become his most loyal servant and personal bodyguard. He was no more than twenty-five, but had a massive physique and was extremely strong and powerful. This strength had been channeled to Mr Sung's own personal welfare, for he had had Victor carefully coached in the oriental martial arts. He was a formidable fighter and yet in the presence of his master he was a gentle giant.

For a moment Mr Sung stared at him, letting his eyes wander freely over his body, then he pulled at the end of his wispy moustache, rubbed the end of his nose and began to speak.

'I have been sent a message of warning, Victor. My Gunk has spoken to me today.'

Victor looked up sharply, avoiding his master's eyes.

'It appears that there is someone who is planning to disrupt our convention. Someone who is coming to us with a heart set on mischief making.'

Victor's eyes opened wide. He was a simple soul, dog-like in his devotion. Mr Sung lowered his voice.

'You must be on the alert, Victor, continually on the alert. It would do us great harm if our world-wide convention attracted bad publicity. As you know, there are many, many people outside our movement who would be glad to see us destroyed. People who say that what we teach is rubbish, that what I proclaim is all lies.' Mr Sung had opened his eyes wide and was staring hard at Victor. The youth was beginning to feel uncomfortable under the intensity of his gaze.

'There are even people who say that I seduce young people into joining this movement under false pretences. That I lure the youth away from their parents. That I come as a divisive force between parents and their children.'

'They abuse you,' muttered Victor.

'They abuse not only me. They abuse the Truth. Now listen carefully, Victor.' Mr Sung had lowered his voice once more. His eyes were now half-closed and he spoke to Victor very slowly and distinctly. 'It may well be that you might see things which you do not immediately understand.'

'How do you mean?'

'It may be that you will notice me having to deal harshly with an individual, possibly in a way which you have never seen before. If you do, you must observe secrecy and discretion and realise that I am dealing with an enemy of the movement. We may even have a traitor in our midst!'

Victor nodded. Mr Sung need never doubt his loyalty. He would remain loyal to the grave – and beyond.

'You need never doubt me,' said Victor. 'Everything you do is inspired from the galaxy.'

Mr Sung smiled and pulled the other end of his moustache. Victor was the complete disciple. The complete, unquestioning disciple, a model Milky Wayfarer.

'There is one thing I should like to ask,' said Victor softly. 'You said, our Father, that you would shortly instruct me in the final attainment ot our faith – the detachment of the soul from the body. When can my instruction begin?'

'As soon as we have the convention behind us,' said Mr Sung without hesitation. 'As soon as we have returned to Hong Kong I will place you in the class of instruction together with the other novices who have reached your advanced stage of development. As soon as we have returned and completed our work here, you will commence the course.'

Victor smiled with pleasure.

'Thank you, our Father,' he said. 'May I go now? I will remember all that you have said.'

'Yes, you may go. Return with my car in one hour. It is only twenty minutes from this hotel to the convention hall. Everyone should be assembled by the time we arrive. Everything should be in order.' Victor got up and walked backwards out of his master's presence.

'Thy will be done,' he muttered.

Precisely one hour later Victor returned and Mr Sung clambered into his silver and gold Mercedes. His religion had made him an extremely wealthy man, a living proof of the power of his Gunk, as he put it.

The Assembly Hall at Pinner seated five hundred and an additional two hundred were able to stand. Mr Sung had chosen this hall for his convention because of its unusual construction which enabled a speaker to be seen quite clearly by everyone inside it. It also enabled the speaker to see each and every member of his audience. An important factor to Mr Sung, whose ability as a speaker to a mass audience was second to none.

Mr Sung's entrance was as dramatic as it was effective. He was met at the entrance to the hall by six high priests, each from a different continent and of a different nationality. Each one was dressed in a pure white robe which was draped like a Roman toga about his body. With the high priests were six girls, all under twenty and dressed in bright pink wrappers and blouses. Their heads were completely covered with white veils. The girls were also from different nationalities but had been selected by Mr

Sung not so much on account of their spiritual development within the religious 'order, but primarily on account of their beauty. Mr Sung liked his religion to be decorative and his female devotees to be feminine.

The welcoming party proceeded to enter the convention hall backwards, quietly clapping their hands in front of them in well-timed unison. This ritual was not, according to Mr Sung, intended to convey adulation of his own presence, but rather to frighten away any evil spirit or influence which might injure his holy presence. However, not unnaturally, a great number of his followers in the main body of the hall did not realise the precise significance of this and took it upon themselves to clap in rapturous applause at the appearance of their leader.

This was, of course, exactly as Mr Sung had intended it to be, and as the crescendo of noise increased, he gave a slight wave of his hand to the left and to the right which only served to heighten the dramatic effect. The procession moved slowly towards a raised platform at the edge of the hall, and the congregation began to chant, 'Our Father. Our Father. Our Father.'

The leading priests followed by the spiritual handmaidens, slowly made their ascent up the six steps which led to the dais and when Mr Sung, with Victor behind him, climbed up these steps, the noise in the convention hall reached a crescendo. When the little Chinaman finally turned and held up both hands in total acknowledgement of his reception, the noise and excitement reached a fever pitch.

Beneath the silk, yellow gown, Mr Sung felt the

pinch of his bullet-proof vest which he had always worn ever since an attack on his life at a convention in the Bahamas three years previously. He had many enemies, not least among the outraged parents of children who had left their homes to live in the communes which the Milky Wayfarers organization had estabished throughout the world.

The high priests and the girls sat down on chairs which had been placed behind Mr Sung's raised dais. Victor, who was dressed in an immaculate white suit, folded his arms and stood by his master's side.

The little man held up his hands once again, but this time turned his palms towards his audience and motioned to them to be silent. This was the moment when he had to assert his authority and to dominate the convention with the extraordinary power which he possessed.

A hush fell on the hall and Mr Sung opened his eyes wide. The lighting had been carefully planned so that a subdued light with a green filter shone directly on to him.

The effect made his green eyes flash with the intensity of precious stone. It was these eyes which he was able to use in the techniques of mass hypnotism which were the secret of Mr Sung's success. He momentarily allowed his eyes to wander over the expectant, upturned faces in front of him. The effect was instantaneous. Every single person in the hall immediately fell under his spell.

His opening words were always the same, but they never ceased to achieve the same electric effect.

'Obey the Law,' chanted Mr Sung.

'The Law is within us,' the audience responded.

'Follow the Path.'

'The Path leads upwards.'
'Into the galaxy.'
'The galaxy of the stars.'
'To find our Womb.'
'The Womb of our Mother.'
'Each and everyone of us.'
'Each and everyone of us.'

'I am your Father,' Mr Sung glared at them daring anyone to defy his outspoken challenge.

'You are our Father,' the Milky Wayfarers shouted back.

His supremacy asserted and unchallenged, Mr Sung flung out his arms and welcomed them unrestrainedly to the convention. 'A time', he said, 'for prayer and meditation. For revelation and in particular for Gunk contact. A time to grow inwardly and spiritually. A time for love.' His audience listened in total and absolute silence. In spite of the numbers in the hall, there was neither a cough nor a whisper. He held them totally enthralled under his hypnotic stare. Half an hour later, having both harangued his audience and praised them. Having urged them to respect their own Gunk above everything else, yes, even above their 'own parents, wives, husbands, or sweethearts,' he came to the most dramatic point of his speech.

'And now brothers and sisters of the galaxy,' he shouted. 'I have the special duty of welcoming a brother to-night who has reached a stage in his development which we can all aspire to, but few indeed will be lucky enough to reach. Our brother, Mister Prince, who inspired our movement in Nigeria, has come to us to-day not in bodily form but in a truly spiritual form. He has left his earthly body behind him but is nevertheless, with us in this hall.' Mr Sung paused and his eyes seemed to flash even more brightly. 'In fact,' he said, his voice dropping for a moment so that his audience had to strain forward to catch each remarkable word which he uttered, 'I am going to introduce him, now.'

A further pause and then a cry from Mr Sung which caused his audience to gasp in amazement.

'Are you with us Brother Prince?'

For a moment there was total silence and then from a point high up in the roof of the hall came the sound of a voice which to those who knew him, was unmistakenly that of Mr Prince.

'I am here, our Father. I am here and I salute you.'

'And where is your body?'

'In my home town in Nigeria. By the end of the convention I will manifest it before you if my Gunk wills it.

'Welcome, Mr Prince. I know that you will make a unique contribution to the convention, your presence here has assured us of that.'

Chapter Six

Pius Shale slowly opened his eyes and immediately was abruptly sick. The drug he had been given was extremely powerful, the side-effects nauseating and the dosage had been sufficient to keep him in a state of total oblivion for over seven hours. He felt ill and extremely weak, he tried to stand but soon realised that he was strapped tightly in a sitting position, possibly in a chair.

He reopened his eyes and this time, although he was again overcome with a feeling of nausea, he was able to control his retching stomach.

He seemed to be imprisoned in total darkness and he struggled to recall the sequence of events which led up to this present situation. He remembered boarding the plane and the battle to do so. He remembered Samson Sigwe. He suddenly remembered accepting the whisky which he now knew was heavily drugged but after that ... total nothingness. He closed his eyes. His head was throbbing unmercifully and his body ached from the rough ropes which bound him to the uncomfortable metal chair. Twenty minutes later he was aware of approaching footsteps. He forced himself to the alert. A bolt was drawn, then another. He heard a lock turn and suddenly the room he was in was flooded with light.

'Throw him in there,' said a cruel voice. 'When we start torturing his nephew in front of him he might feel obliged to speak.'

There was a thud as a heavy object crashed to the ground.

'Is the other one awake yet?'

Pius felt a heavy hand on his shoulder and he feigned unconsciousness.

'No, it doesn't look like it. Give them a couple of hours and we'll have them both singing like birds.'

The light was extinguished, the door slammed shut. Even though his brain was dulled, Pius knew that the new occupant of his prison must be the person who he had originally set out to look for – Mr Prince. He also knew that his own true identity had still not been revealed. There was utter silence for a moment and then the person who had been thrown into the room let out an agonised groan.

What have they been doing to him, thought Pius. Beating him up? But if so, why? He was supposed to be one of them.

Ten minutes later after a further succession of groans, Pius knew that Mr Prince was regaining consciousness.

'Mr Prince,' Pius whispered. 'Is your name, Mr Prince?' For a moment there was utter silence and then a weary voice said quite distinctly, 'Who are you? What do you want with me?'

Slowly and carefully, Pius managed to explain to the man just who he was, who their captors thought he was and why he was here. Mr Prince, who had not yet been beaten up but who had been subjected to intensely hostile questioning, managed to explain to Pius that he had been kidnapped in Nigeria and brought to the UK at the command of Mr Sung.

'Are we in England?' asked Pius. 'I don't know where we are. For all I know my flight might never have taken off and we could still be in Nigeria.'

'No, we are definitely in the UK,' replied Mr Prince grimly. 'I was brought here by force when I told Mr Sung that I was going to come to the convention by my own unconventional means.'

'Yes, I heard all about that from Missis Queen.'

'Oh, I can do it,' muttered Mr Prince. 'I can certainly leave my body and travel. That's the cause of the trouble.'

'What do you mean?'

'I have the secret, I can do it, and Mr Sung is most anxious to acquire that secret for himself.'

'Are you serious?' asked Pius, who was rapidly managing to shake off the effects of his drugs under the stimulus of their conversation.

'Absolutely.'

'But Queen told me that you were an ardent Milky Wayfarer. Why do you not want to reveal your secret to the organisation when you are one of their passionate followers?'

'Because I happened to find out something quite by chance. Something which suddenly made me realise that the whole organisation run by Mr Sung is a fraud, a lie. A brutal and wicked lie.'

'What do you mean?'

'What I mean is that Mr Sung has convinced his thousands of young followers that the Milky Way-farers possess the ultimate secret, the secret of spirit travel.'

60

'Well, isn't that what you say you possess?' demanded Pius.

'But I can do it. I can do it, yet not one of them, not even Mr Sung himself, has the slightest idea how to achieve it.'

'Which is why they were so interested in you as an active member?'

'Exactly, and it is also the reason why they kidnapped me and brought me here by force. Some of the younger members in the organisation are beginning to question the findings and beliefs of Mr Sung. In spite of his undoubted power as a hypnotist, some people are beginning to reaslise that what he was teaching them was based on a pack of lies. Just a great deal of nonsense. Suddenly Mr Sung saw me as an escape from his predicament. I was the one person who could give their whole movement credibility; provided they had my secret.'

'And have they got it out of you?' asked Pius anxiously. 'Did you give it to them?'

'No, I gave them something which they will soon discover is just nonsense. I let them tape record my voice so that Sung could fool all those people in the convention hall that I was really floating about over their heads. But they haven't got the real formula – and they never will have it,' he insisted grimly.

'They still think that I am your nephew,' said Pius thoughtfully. 'At least, they do for the moment. Unless they are incredibly stupid they won't be thinking that for long.'

'But when they discover that I have given them a load of meaningless jargon, I suspect that they will begin to practice much more unpleasant methods on us to extract the information that they are looking for,' said Prince quietly.

'But why does he do it? Why does Sung spend all his time misleading people in a false religion? Is it just to bolster up his own sense of power or is there another reason?'

'I don't know. That's something I just don't understand. Mr Sung is the only one who can answer that question.' Prince groaned and strained at his ropes. 'How are we going to get out of here? Somehow we have got to escape.'

Pius had already been thinking of a plan. 'Are your teeth any good, Mr Prince?'

'Yes. Why?'

'Well, if I can manage to tip my chair over so that it falls near where you are lying, maybe you could manage to start attacking my knots with your teeth and I could do the same to yours. It's the only chance we've got, unless . . .'

'Unless what?'

'Unless you manage to leave your body and come over here and untie me,' said Pius with a short laugh.

'Not a chance,' said Mr Prince. 'I need to take the right medicine beforehand.'

'Well, if that's the case, it had better be my plan,' said Pius, starting to rock his chair sideways. 'I can't see you, but I know approximately where you are lying. With a bit of luck . . .' Pius crashed to the floor trapping his fingers under the metal supports of his chair. He fought back the pain and gritted his teeth. 'Where are you, Prince?'

'Right beside you. That was clever.'

'No so clever for my fingers' sake,' said Pius grimly. 'I hope I didn't damage my watch.'

'Why?'

'It's the only weapon I have.'

'Please explain.'

'Explanations later. Come on, Prince, if we leave it too late those devils will be back here to beat us up.'

The two men edged together and indicated to each other where their knots were positioned. They had been expertly tied up and after ten minutes of futile progress, it was clear that they were getting nowhere. Pius was nearing dispair when he suddenly felt with his cheek something small and hard in the pocket of Prince's jacket.

'Are those matches?'

'Yes.'

'Do you think I can get them out of your pocket? If we can manage to strike a match then maybe we can burn through the rope. We will never get those knots undone with our teeth.'

Pius buried his face in Prince's jacket and began to pull at the pocket with his teeth. After two minutes of frantic effort, the pocket suddenly tore and he managed to pick up the matchbox. He gently pushed at the end with his tongue and forced the box open.

'Can you get a match out with your teeth, Prince? If I shake them on to your face?'

'I'll try.'

Pius shook the box vigorously and after a few seconds the matches tumbled down on to Prince who managed to grip one between his teeth. Pius strained forward in an effort to hold the striking edge of the box out to him and the two men spent an uncomfortable few minutes struggling to ignite a match. Pius knew that they could well ignite each others hair unless they were very careful. Suddenly the match burst into flame and Pius jerked his head rapidly away.

'Quickly, try and burn through the piece of rope which is round my arm.'

Prince pushed his head forward and for an agonising few seconds held the match under the rope. The match suddenly went out, but Pius knew from the dull glow and the smell of burning that the rope was smouldering.

'Well done, Prince,' said Pius. 'Well done. Now, if it will only stay alight.'

The glow spread and the smoke intensified. Pius strained to force the strands apart. With dramatic suddenness, the rope suddenly snapped.

'We've done it,' Pius muttered. He forced his freed hand apart and started to pick furiously at the knot on his other wrist. A few minutes later he was free and releasing Mr Prince. The two men sat for a moment rubbing their chafed and aching limbs. Then Pius struck another match and surveyed his companion. His dark suit was ripped and torn, and his face was cut and puffed out on one side. In spite of this, Mr Prince, who was younger than Pius had expected him to be, seemed alert and ready for action.

'They have been knocking you about,' whispered Pius. 'You look as though they did beat you up.'

'They were somewhat rough with me. They tore my jacket to see if I had a written note of the formula, but it is all in my head.'

Suddenly Pius remembered the note which Bisi had given to him in Lagos. He mentally kicked himself for forgetting about it for so long. He reached into his coat pocket. To his dismay the pocket was torn – the note had disappeared. He cursed softly to himself, remembering how his jacket had been ripped in the flight to get on board flight 800. What had she been trying to tell me? he wondered.

Further speculation was abruptly cut short by the sound of approaching footsteps. Pius's heart started to beat loudly. Their captors were not leaving them alone for long.

'What shall we do?' whispered Prince desperately. 'What can we do?'

'Lie down in the exact position you were in on the floor,' whispered Pius back at him. 'Throw those ropes over yourself and try to make it seem as though you are still tied up. Wait for my order before you do anything. Just shut your eyes, don't move and pray.'

Pius quietly put his chair back into its original position and tucked his own ropes around him as best he could. No sooner had he done so, than he heard the bolts on the door being drawn back and the turn of a key in the lock. He knew there was more than one man.

The door was flung noisily open and the room was suddenly flooded in light. Pius let his head slump forward as though he was still under the influence of the drugged whisky.

'He seems to be sleeping on,' said a voice. 'It's about time we woke him up.' Pius waited and listened as the man who had spoken strode over towards him. He stood in front of Pius and slapped him viciously. 'Wake up, you. We need to talk.'

Pius reacted instantly. His right hand had been folded over his left and, as the man hit him, he pressed a small button on the side of his digital watch. Instantly, a thick stream of fluid shot straight into the face of his attacker who screamed in agony. 'My face is on fire! My eyes! Oh, my eyes!' The man staggered away from Pius. Meanwhile, his companion had rushed over to give assistance. As he stood for a second over Pius, uncertain what to do, Pius pressed the little button once again and a second squirt of the deadly fluid sprayed into the man's face.

65

'Aaah,' the man shrieked, staggering backwards. 'I can't see.'

He raised his hands to his face and, as he did so, Pius sprang from the chair and hit him hard in the stomach. The man slumped to the ground, his hands tearing wildly at his eyes. The first victim was still staggering helplessly about.

'Quick, Prince, stuff something in their mouths,' shouted Pius as he dealt the other man a savage blow on the back of the neck. He slumped to the ground as Prince started to stuff a handkerchief into the mouth of the groaning figure who was writhing on the floor.

Pius was already starting to tie the two men up with the ropes which had been used on Prince and himself. He used a method which he believed would preclude escape, tying their necks back firmly to their bound feet. The slightest struggle would jerk their heads backwards into an agonising position. The two men's eyes were streaming, inflamed and bloodshot. Pius tore a piece of cloth from the bottom of his shirt and gagged them both. When they were totally secure, he rolled them to opposite sides of the room to ensure that they could have no contact with one another.

He looked at Prince who was staring at him in amazement.

'Who taught you to fight like that?' Prince gasped, 'And what was it that you sprayed into their faces?'

'I knew my little present from my colleague, Bisi, would come in useful before long,' said Pius, patting what seemed to be an inexpensive digital watch. 'This watch is not very special, Prince, but it contains one extra button, a button which releases a shot of the venom of the spitting cobra! They won't be blinded for ever, but neither of those two crooks will be seeing straight for at least a fortnight.'

Prince looked admiringly on as Pius ran over to the men and turned out their jacket and trouser pockets. The only thing he removed from one of them was a set of car keys.

Suddenly a thought struck him, he stopped and turned to Prince. 'Where did you say you were kidnapped?' he demanded.

'In my home town, Asaba.'

'And how did they do it?'

'They drugged me in the same way as they drugged you.'

'And then what?'

'I woke up here. In this very room. In exactly the same way as you did. After that they took me for an interview with Mr Sung.'

'Was that far away from here?'

'No, not at all. It only took twenty minutes or so by car.'

'I don't understand,' said Pius, whistling softly to himself.

'What don't you understand, please?'

'Well, you were drugged and brought forcibly over here. I was drugged and brought unconscious out of our country.'

'So?'

'Don't you see, Prince? Samson and his accomplice, Luka, managed to bring me through the British passport control and customs without apparently any problems at all. It's not easy you know. How do you get a drugged person into this country unless an official somewhere is turning a mighty blind eye to this situation? And they managed to perform this miracle not only once, but twice!'

67

Chapter Seven

'Have we got it, Samson? Have we got what we are after?' Mr Sung fixed his eyes firmly on Samson Sigwe. Samson looked quickly away.

'No, our Father. The traitor gave us something and we mixed it up, but it is worthless, utterly worthless, just a recipe for making nonsense.' Samson Sigwe shuffled uneasily under the menacing glare of the Chinaman. 'I have sent two of our heavies to Primrose Gardens to rough him up and that nephew of his, Julius.'

Mr Sung's eyes narrowed. 'You are failing me, Samson Sigwe,' he said in a whisper. 'You are failing me. Do you realise that? You have at very high risk brought two men out of their country quite successfully and against their will, and yet you are unable to extract the information which is vital to the continued success of our movement.'

Samson said nothing and continued to stare down at his feet.

Suddenly Mr Sung erupted like a smouldering volcano. 'You are a fool, an idiot, an incompetent,

Samson. You have committed a blunder of gigantic proportions.'

Samson looked up in utter bewilderment. 'I have tried, our Father, I have tried . . .'

'Tried, you idiot?' the little man screamed at him. 'Tried? Do you know what you have done? You have been duped. That so-called nephew of Prince happens to be a private detective, a special agent, and you have brought him right into our midst.'

'But . . .' Samson began to protest.

'Don't but me. Your so-called Julius Prince was carrying a hold-all which no doubt you searched?'

'Yes, of course.'

Mr Sung's eyes glowed. 'Yes, of course. Yes, of course you did. In your own most inefficient manner. Luckily Victor is able to do things somewhat more thoroughly than you. He found a secret compartment in your Mr Prince's nephew's hold-all. He found certain instructions.'

For a moment the little Chinaman stopped shaking and reaching into his embroidered gown pulled out Queen's written instructions. 'Take them. Read them, you blundering fool, and then take my congratulations for introducing special agent, Pius Shale, into our midst.'

Samson took the papers and read them slowly and thoughtfully. 'But he was on our trail anyway,' he said slowly, after a moment's pause. 'He was coming to us, our Father.'

'Yes, I know, I know. But we didn't have to drug him and bring him directly into our circle. He has most likely come round now and is, no doubt, talking to his "dear uncle" at number 49, Primrose Gardens.'

'I have already sent two of our men round there. They

will do whatever you want them to do.'

Mr Sung paused, and then slowly raised a hand and extended it towards Samson, pointing at him with his index finger.

'Look at me, Samson Sigwe.'

Samson raised his eyes and, as they met those of the Chinaman, they started to glaze over.

'Are you looking at me, Samson Sigwe?'

'Yes, our Father.'

'Can you feel my power sweeping over you, taking hold of you?'

'Yes, our Father.'

'You know what you have to do, don't you, Samson?'

'Yes, our Father.'

'What do you have to do, Samson Sigwe?'

'I, I,' Samson faltered for an instant.

'Yes, go on.'

'I have to kill Pius Shale.'

'That is correct, quite correct. And what is more you must do it quickly and discreetly. He must be eliminated and disposed of. The authorities here did not see him enter this country.'

'That is correct.'

'Well, in that case they will be none the wiser when he is disposed of. You have a method?'

'Yes, our Father.'

'Good. Don't tell me. I hate the sordid, messy side of things. After all,' he added, turning away from Samson for a moment, 'our religion is one of love and brotherhood, is that not so?'

'Yes, our Father.'

'Good, well go, and do our will.'

'Yes, our Father.'

'One further thing before you go.' The green eyes of

Mr Sung swept once more over the face of Samson Sigwe, found his eyes and held them firmly in his gaze. 'I have told you countless times before that we must have that formula from Prince. Our whole movement must have it. The Wayfarers whole ethos is built on spirit travel. We have the power to achieve that very thing. It is within our grasp. You must not fail to extract the secret from that stubborn, traitorous man. Even if at the end of your questioning he too has to be silenced for ever.'

Samson Sigwe mumbled his assent once more.

'If Victor, or anyone else outside our inner circle, finds out that we do not possess this secret, then, my friend, it will be you who will make a permanent disappearance from this earth and rapidly become reunited with your Gunk. Even now some members are daring to ask embarrassing questions. Do I make myself absolutely and utterly clear?'

'Yes, our Father.'

'Good. Then in your Gunk's name, go.'

Samson Sigwe left the room backwards and quietly closed the door. Mr Sung reached for the internal phone and summoned Victor to his room. A few minutes later Victor appeared.

'That man, Samson Sigwe, Victor, you are friends? After all, he is your countryman.'

'We are all taught to love our brothers,' said Victor obediently.

Mr Sung paused for a moment. 'Quite true, Victor,' he said, 'But if our brothers fail in their duties, especially when they have reached the status of high priest, then they have to be watched very carefully. Do you understand me, Victor?'

'I am not sure, our father.'

'Victor, look at me.'

71

The youth started to protest, but he was caught up in Mr Sung's intensive gaze.

'Watch him. Watch him very carefully, Victor, very carefully indeed. If you ever suspect him of not being loyal to our movement, then he will have to have an accident that will put him out of action – permanently. You will have to see that the accident happens, Victor.'

Victor, who was now totally under the other man's hypnotic spell, nodded his head vigorously up and down. Seemingly satisfied, Mr Sung relaxed. 'Good, Victor, you are my most loyal disciple. Now then, I have become so distracted with my problems that I am unaware of either the time or this evening's timetable. Refresh my memory please.'

'This evening at five the second session of the convention begins. Private study groups and Gunk prayer meetings. You are due to meet the high priests at nine o'clock to prepare them for tomorrow's divine instruction on practical spirituality.'

'And the time now?'

'Three twenty.'

'Good, Victor. Call me in precisely one hour and we will proceed together to the convention. I wish to be left alone for an hour. I feel the time is good for Gunk contact and I need advice from my mother spirit. I suggest you go and do the same, Victor.'

'Yes, our Father,' said Victor, backing silently out of the room and closing the door discreetly behind him. Mr Sung listened until his footsteps had died completely away and then he moved rapidly back to the telephone.

'Hallo, reception? Ah good, I want a New York number. Can you please call 010 1 212 622724?' There was a pause. Mr Sung looked nervously around him as though half afraid that someone might be in the room with him.

'Hallo? Williamson?' he said suddenly. 'Is that you? Good. This is our Father. Can you hear me distinctly? You can? Good. Now, listen, Williamson, a high priest is coming your way with good news. He has been spiritually enlightened and is coming to spread our message. Did you hear all that? Good. He hopes to travel on Thursday's flight from Heathrow, PANAM 789, and he will have met flight 800. You will see he is met? OK? Good. Bye, Williamson, and good luck with your missionaries.'

Mr Sung gently replaced the receiver and taking a faded yellow cloth from out of the depths of his embroidered gown, carefully mopped his brow. He gave a little sigh, squatted down on a pile of cushions which Victor had carefully placed in the centre of the floor and composed himself for meditation.

Meanwhile Victor, with an hour to spare before he called his master, had walked down the stairs and into the entrance hall of the small hotel. Mr Sung had chosen both the hotel and the assembly hall very carefully. They were both discreetly hidden away in an obscure London suburb. The very last thing he had wanted to do was to attract attention from the British press. Had he hired a large hall in the centre of London and stayed in an expensive and flamboyant hotel, he would have done just that, and anyway, he also wanted to be conveniently situated for Heathrow Airport.

Victor smiled at the attractive girl behind the reception desk. 'Hallo.'

'Hallo,' the girl replied. 'Are you off somewhere?'

'Nowhere in particular,' said Victor, 'just killing time.'

'Why don't we kill it together?' the girl said, half closing her eyes. 'I am off duty in ten minutes.'

Victor turned away. 'Sorry, I can't . . .'

Suddenly the girl flared up. 'What's wrong with you Nigerians?' she asked huffily. 'Don't you like talking to girls or something? Why, I started to talk to another of your countrymen just now and he said that he had to go off somewhere and had no time.'

'Another Nigerian? Which one?'

'Oh, Sam something or other,' the girl continued wearily. 'What's it to you? You have all got no time.' She turned her back on Victor who strode over to her desk.

'You mean the man called Samson?'

'Could be.'

'Has he just gone somewhere?'

'Primrose Gardens, I think it was. What's it to you, anyway? You're all the same, no time.'

Even as the girl uttered these last words, Victor was already moving through the hotel swing-door. He knew number 49, Primrose Gardens, and he knew that Mr Sung had hired it as additional accommodation for the convention. What he did not know was that it had been used as a prison to hold Pius and Prince. Mr Sung had wisely kept the loyal Victor in total ignorance of this and other more worldly matters' that the movement pursued.

As Victor jogged the short distance to 49, Primrose Gardens, one thought was uppermost in his mind. If Samson Sigwe had ignored the overtures of a pretty girl, then clearly he had something very important to do. For Samson's weakness for the female sex had been responsible for his being at cross purposes with Mr Sung on other occasions before now, and in various places in the world. Samson placed girls high on his

74

priority list. To have had this priority ousted by something even more important was something which made Victor highly suspicious that he was up to no good.

He ran rapidly through the quiet residential streets oblivious of the glances of a few passers-by which were cast in the direction of the immaculately dressed and muscular youth. When he reached 49, Primrose Gardens, the first thing he noticed was that the front door was slightly ajar, and that all the curtains in the house were firmly drawn although it was only afternoon and still quite light. He slowed to a walk and stealthily approached the entrance. He pushed the door open and quietly slipped inside the house.

Everything was dark except for a shaft of light which shone from an upstairs room. He crept up the stairs, walked along the narrow landing and peered round the door and into the room from which the light was shining.

What he saw made him gasp in horror. Samson Sigwe was bending over a man and struggling with a rope which seemed to secure him. The man was groaning, and another man, whom Victor instantly recognised as one of Mr Sung's high priests, was lying similarly trussed at the other side of the room.

Victor neither stopped to question nor to think. The injunction to keep a special watch on Samson Sigwe had been firmly planted in his mind less than half an hour previously. It was an injunction to kill if necessary and here was the very man he had been told to watch caught in the act of tying up two of his own spiritual brothers.

Without uttering a word, Victor ran over to Samson and pulled him roughly to his feet. Although Samson himself was physically strong, he had been so intent on

75

trying to release the two prisoners that he was oblivious of Victor's presence until the last minute.

'Why, Victor, what ...?'

The sentence was cut short as Victor dealt him a crashing blow to the jaw. As Samson reeled backwards with a cry of 'fool' on his lips, Victor caught hold of his coat lapel and pulled him forward. He raised his arm and brought it sharply down on the nape of his neck in a classical exhibition of a Chinese chop. Samson Sigwe slumped to the floor.

Chapter Eight

Bisi stared hard at the Nigeria High Commission's First Secretary, Mr Daniel Owusu. 'Are you sure?' she asked. 'Are you quite sure that there has not been a message left for me?'

'Quite sure,' said Daniel, staring up at his attractive visitor and wagging his head from side to side. 'And what is more, I have checked with everyone from the High Commissioner downwards. There has been neither a message nor a telephone call.'

'But that's strange,' said Bisi. 'I told him in my note to contact you on arrival and either to meet me here or leave a message.'

Bisi frowned and sat down in the comfortable chair which was placed some way away from the desk of the First Secretary. The message had been perfectly clear. She had given it to Pius at the airport, and she knew that if he hadn't been able to get here he would have sent a message of some description – unless he had got into some sort of trouble.

'I expect he couldn't make it,' said Mr Owusu helpfully.

'No,' said Bisi firmly, 'that's not the way we work. If we can't meet each other, we always get in touch.'

'Anyway,' said Mr Owusu brightly, 'did you have a good trip over here?'

'Yes, fine, fine,' said Bisi. 'No problem. It was a smooth flight, no overbook, no palaver. I think the only thing they forgot to do was to put the pepper and salt out when they gave us our meal. But the meal was very good and so that didn't matter.'

'Good for flight 800?'

'Yes, indeed,' said Bisi, 'At least we didn't have the technical hitch which Pius had twenty-four hours earlier. By the way,' she said, glancing up sharply at the man seated behind the desk, 'have you checked out Mr Sung and his crazy organisation?'

'Yes,' replied Mr Owusu. 'We have got a great deal from Interpol and also some back-up information of our own from Lagos.'

'OK, let's have it.'

Mr Owusu pulled out a file from his top drawer marked 'Secret'. It was tied to a sheaf of photographs with a bright red ribbon. He undid the bow and handed the photographs to Bisi. 'Take a look at those before I give you the background.'

Bisi said nothing, but took the photographs from his outstretched hand. 'So this is Mr Sung, the oriental mystic,' she said eventually. 'Does he always wear that extraordinary yellow robe?'

'So we are told. Never been seen dressed in anything else.'

'And this?'

'That's Samson Sigwe. Sung's right hand man back

home. Ex-"biafran" lieutenant turned religious.'

'He doesn't look the religious type to me,' said Bisi. 'Looks more like a small-time crook.'

'There's nothing on him,' said the First Secretary. 'We checked him out very thoroughly with Lagos. A complete nonentity during the civil war and apart from a visit to Hong Kong under the wing of Mr Sung, he does not appear to have left Nigeria.'

'Until now.'

'Until now,' said Mr Owusu, correcting himself with a smile. 'Until his attendance at the convention.'

'But we know he was on flight 800 together with Pius and a colleague of his called Luka. I myself saw them all go through security.'

'Correct, but Pius wasn't with them. Our information says he passed through security on his own.'

'That's true, but I saw him talking to them earlier and it struck me that Mr Sigwe had suddenly become very interested in Pius Shale.'

Bisi had turned over the photograph of a young and attractive girl who seemed to be about twenty-eight years old.

'And who is this?' she asked. 'She looks like a hot little number.'

'That's Comfort Ademoga. She is a handmaiden, quite a high up one in the Milky Wayfarers.'

'A handmaiden? What do you mean? Please explain yourself, Daniel.'

Mr Owusu had opened his file and was slowly turning the pages. He paused and ran his finger quickly down a page. 'The Milky Wayfarers have two offices in their cult,' he read, 'high priests for men and handmaidens for women. These act as the senior officials in each country where there are members of the sect. They coordinate the activities of the religion within their country and are directly responsible to Mr Sung himself. The high priests deal with the males in each country and the handmaidens with the females. There are no other officials and these handpicked organisers are sent on a course of instruction after their selection.'

'Which is why Samson went to Hong Kong?' said Bisi.

'Exactly, and it appears that Comfort accompanied him on that particular trip.'

'So Comfort is the head of our women in the movement and Samson is in charge of the men. How many followers are there?'

'Not many. The figures have been grossly exaggerated. We don't think that there are more than two hundred women and three hundred men in the whole of our country.'

'But that's nothing,' said Bisi. 'What about here in England?'

'Even less. This movement is very, very small which is why neither the press nor the police are paying much attention to their convention which is now going on in Pinner. But the spread is great.'

'What do you mean?'

'Well, although the numbers are small, Sung seems to have followers in a good number of African and Asian countries, as well as here in the West.'

'Eastern Europe?'

'Not to our knowledge.'

'And is this Prince? The man who started this wild goose chase? The man who can float through space? The cause of all our problems.'

'That's your man.'

'He seems harmless enough to me.'

'He is, as far as we know. Just an ordinary herbalist who got caught up with the sect because his discoveries coincides with their theories.'

Bisi continues to stare at the picture of the neat, dapper little man from Asaba, a strange companion for the mighty Queen, she thought to herself.

'OK, Daniel,' Bisi said authoritatively, 'so much for this rogue's gallery. Now for some facts, please, because I am very worried about this lack of communication from Pius. Fact one, where is this convention being held?'

'In Pinner, which is a small suburb of London about ten miles to the west of here.'

'Fact two, how long does it go on for?' Bisi had a small notebook out and was writing his answers down in shorthand, word for word.

'This is the third and last day. They had a rally on the first day at the Pinner Assembly Hall which they hired for the purpose. Then yesterday, it appears they had prayer meetings and Gunk contact.'

'I have heard all about that from Queen,' said Bisi with a grin.

'In the evening they had a meeting of the High Priests at Mr Sung's hotel.'

'Which is?'

'The Royal Court, Oriental Road, Pinner.'

'Sounds appropriate,' said Bisi. 'Were the hand-maidens there?'

'Apparently not. Interpol had a man watching the hotel and they did not appear.'

'So they don't stay at the hotel?'

'No, they are all lodged in another hotel about a mile away called the Rising Sun.'

'Equally appropriate. Is Sung on his own?'

'Yes, apart from Victor.'

'Victor? Who is he?'

'He is an orphan from Lagos who Sung took under his wing some years ago. He enjoys a sort of master/slave relationship with Sung. We understand he is very strong and also acts as Sung's personal bodyguard.'

'Right, I have got all that,' said Bisi when she had finished writing the information down. 'Now, what's on the menu for today?'

'The final rally at eight this evening. Due to last three hours, and as an extra attraction, will feature a flying display by Prince and company.'

'What do you mean, a flying display?'

'I was joking,' said Daniel with a laugh. 'But this is to be Sung's big display, the definite proof of spirit travel, the revelation of the secret of Gunk power.'

'Sounds absolutely crazy to me,' said Bisi.

'It is, but there we are. You can fool some of the people some of the time,' said Mr Owusu with a laugh. 'So, Bisi, you have the facts. What's your plan?'

Bisi sat silent for a few moments, thoughtfully reading back to herself the notes which she had just made. 'If only I knew where Pius was, things would be much easier,' she said. 'I only hope that he hasn't got himself into trouble. He has a nose for that sort of thing, you know.'

'I do know a bit about Pius Shale,' said Daniel with a wink. 'But his past record suggests that he is also very good at getting out of trouble as well as getting into it.'

'With a little help from me from time to time,' said Bisi modestly. 'But as for my plan, Daniel, I think I am going to stick to my own sex and tackle the lady.' She picked up the photograph of the attractive Comfort Ademoga and stared hard at it for a moment. 'She might be pliable. I think she might be pliable.' Bisi held out her right hand and rubbed her fingers together.

'I see what you mean,' said Daniel slowly, 'but we have very little on her. She was only brought into the movement nine months ago and was rapidly made a handmaiden on account of her exceptional ability.'

'Ability to do what?' asked Bisi, staring hard at Mr Owusu. 'That's what concerns me, Daniel. Is it her religious ability or something else?'

'You will have to find that out for yourself,' said Daniel. 'As I say, we have nothing on her at all.'

'That's exactly what I intend to do,' said Bisi, standing up and smoothing her skirt down. 'I suggest you ask the British police to send a few extra coppers round to the assembly hall at Pinner tonight. Just in case we uncover something bigger than we can handle.'

'No chance,' said Daniel shrugging his shoulders. 'They will say we have nothing to go on and that the sect is harmless. They are not at all interested and say that they are far too busy to worry about a crazy Chinaman.'

'OK,' said Bisi, 'then Pius and I will have to handle the matter ourselves in our own individual way. Keep the night line open, Daniel. I may be making urgent contact later on this evening.'

Bisi stood up and with a brief bow in the direction of Daniel Owusu hurried out of his office, down the large staircase of the Nigeria High Commission and out into the busy London street. She hailed a taxi and minutes later was speeding towards Pinner and the hotel called the Rising Sun.

It was six o'clock when she knocked on the door of Room 31, the room occupied by Miss Comfort

Ademoga of the Milky Wayfarers. There was no reply and she knocked softly once again. She was not expecting a reply as the hotel receptionist had already informed her that Miss Ademoga had left the hotel that morning and had not yet returned. On the pretext of going to the toilet, Bisi had slipped up the back stairs to check on the accuracy of this statement for herself.

She knocked a third time and placed her ear to the door. There was complete and utter silence. She reached into her shoulder-bag and extracted a key. It was a very valuable key which had enabled her to investigate a great number of secrets which had been concealed behind closed doors in the past. She was certain that it would not fail her now. Fashioned by an international safe-breaker, whom she and Pius had helped to apprehend, it had an adjustable and utterly flexible mechanism which enabled it to open any known hotel lock in the world. Room number 31 at the Rising Sun, Pinner proved no exception, and seconds later she gently pushed open the door.

She quietly closed it behind her and looked around the room. Comfort's things were placed neatly on the furniture in an unexpectedly orderly fashion, but what immediately caught Bisi's eye was the brightly coloured blouse and wrapper which lay folded on the single bed together with a heavy white veil. She felt the richly embroidered and very expensive material. She thought to herself that handmaidens wore very pretty and . . . a plan was beginning to form in her mind, a plan which was not only daring and audacious but which might enable her to penetrate the innermost secrets of the Milky Wayfarers and discover just what exactly had happened to Mr Prince and Pius.

She went over towards a pile of papers and books on

the table beside the bed. Passport, health documents, the papers seemed in order. The visa to Hong Kong confirmed what Daniel had told her about the visit last year. A letter from a boyfriend back home. She opened it and quickly digested the contents – it seemed that he was begging her to give up the sect because of the dangers involved. Dangers? What dangers? thought Bisi. It may be crazy; but dangerous? The boyfriend had clearly not got a very great hold on Comfort because she was patently ignoring his advice.

She moved over to the smart leather suitcase placed on a trestle table on one side of the room. Clothes, not many but expensive, make-up a lot and equally expensive, powerful scent, a little plastic packet of salt and pepper, a packet of sugar all from flight 800. Now what on earth could she want . . . ? She must have known of the coming shortage, thought Bisi with a grin. A Bible? A Bible? Now that's way out of context. This girl with a Bible? She should be carrying the thoughts of the good Gunk Sung, not a Bible. She opened the Bible and read an inscription on the flyleaf: 'To dear, Comfort. I have marked the passages which lend credibility to our claims, with love Samson.'

Did Samson also chase Comfort, she mused? Further speculation on Bisi's part was suddenly and abruptly halted. A key was starting to turn in the lock. It appeared that Miss Comfort Ademoga was about to make an entrance herself.

..

Chapter Nine

Once outside 49, Primrose Gardens Pius was in no doubt as to what he and Prince must do next. Anxious as he was to have a confrontation with Mr Sung, he knew that the hottest trail to follow must lead to Heathrow Airport. He was certain that there was someone there who must be very adept at getting passengers through immigration, whatever their state of health or mind, and Pius was most anxious to discover who it was. He quickly hailed a taxi and forty minutes later they were sitting in the office of the airport security police inspector who was listening to their respective stories with a minimum of interest.

'You mean to tell me that both you gentlemen were drugged and brought through immigration and customs without being apprehended in any way?' asked the inspector in total disbelief.

'We do,' said Pius who was rapidly growing impatient at the man's inability to grasp the urgency of the situation.

'And you came over yesterday on the Sunshine

Airways flight from Lagos?'

'I did. Mr Prince here was brought forcibly over the day before. The flight number in both cases was 800 and both of us were heavily drugged.'

'Sounds impossible to me,' said the inspector looking Pius slowly up and down. 'You are not trying to pull a fast one on me, are you?'

'No,' said Pius in exasperation at the man's apparent stupidity. 'I am not. I happen to be a special agent.' He pulled out his identity card and thrust it under the inspector's nose. The inspector took it and carefully made a note of the details.

'I'll have to check this out with Lagos,' he said eventually, holding Pius's identity card with obvious disapproval.

'Do what you like. All I want is your co-operation.'

'In what way?'

'I believe today's flight from Lagos is due in shortly. I want to be given authority to be allowed out on to the tarmac and to be given free access to the Sunshine Airways service facility areas.'

'On what grounds?' said the man testily. 'We'll have to check you out first.'

'Look, there is no time,' Pius shouted at him. 'Can't you understand the meaning of the word? I have been drugged, my friend here has been kidnapped against his will. I believe that there is something odd about flight 800 from Nigeria, and by the time you get a reply on the telex, it could be back in the air heading for home.'

'Telex is instantaneous,' said the inspector wearily. 'I will soon check you out.'

'You don't know my country,' said Pius firmly. 'Look, there's a phone here. Can I phone my High Commission in London?'

'If you must.'

Pius dialled the number and within minutes was speaking to Daniel Owusu. 'Is that you, Pius? Why haven't you rung in earlier? Bisi is getting most anxious about you.'

'Bisi? Over here in the UK? But I didn't know...'

'She said she gave you a note at Lagos airport.'

'It went astray,' said Pius ruefully. 'It went astray before I even boarded the plane. So that's what Bisi wanted me to do, contact her over here!'

'Yes, and she has been exceedingly worried because you failed to do just that.'

'Where is she now?'

'She has gone to the Milky Wayfarer's convention at the Assembly Hall, Pinner, at least that was her plan before she left here.'

The inspector who had been listening to Pius's end of the conversation was growing restless. 'I thought you were going to let me speak to someone who would check you out,' he interrupted impatiently. 'It appears you are more interested in talking to your friend.'

Pius controlled himself and said, 'Daniel, there is a guy here who doesn't believe what I tell him. He didn't even believe his own eyes when he saw my little blue plastic pass. Do you think you could settle his mind for him? I need someone's permission to sniff around the airport when flight 800 rolls in.'

Pius passed the receiver over to the security inspector. Five minutes later he had been reluctantly convinced that Pius was indeed what he made himself out to be. He handed the telephone back to Pius.

'Oh, Daniel,' said Pius. 'Just before you go. If Bisi rings in, please tell her where I am and what I am up to.'

'I won't know what you are up to, just as I won't

know what she is up to,' said Mr Owusu with a laugh, 'but I will try and tell her just the same. Take care though, Pius, it seems to me that there may be a big fish in your particular stretch of water.'

'I will. Good-bye, Daniel.' Pius replaced the receiver and turned to the inspector. 'Now may I have your permission to have free access to any part of the airport?'

The inspector did not reply but walked over to a large safe standing in one corner of his office. He opened it and removed a small plastic pass which he signed, dated and stamped. He then handed it to Pius.

'Here you are, this will be sufficient for your purpose. It is a special and does not require your photograph. What is your companion going to do?' he continued, pointing towards Mr Prince who had been sitting quietly on his own. 'If you wish, he can remain with me in this office, but I am afraid he cannot have an authorisation to accompany you.'

'You will be all right here,' Pius said to Mr Prince who seemed quite content to remain where he was. He was relieved he was not going to have Prince by his side. This was the kind of job where he much preferred to act on his own. 'I want to watch the crew disembark. So it will be over an hour and a half before I get back. Why don't you explain to our friend here how you can fly solo?'

Pius slipped quickly out of the office before Prince had a chance to reply. The first thing he had to do was to find out exactly where the loading bay for Sunshine Airways was situated. The more he thought about it, the more he felt convinced that neither Prince nor himself had left the plane by normal channels. No immigration or customs authority in the world would have turned a blind eye to a drugged person being wheeled or carried past them. They must have been brought off the plane by another method.

An airport official gave Pius the necessary directions after he had shown him his newly acquired special pass, and ten minutes later he entered the Sunshine Airways loading and unloading bay. This was used, not for passengers' luggage, but for the loading and removal of food and drink for the flight, and for storing in-flight sales goods. It appeared that the only other person in the area was a Pakistani lady cleaner who smiled mournfully at Pius as he entered, and continued with her half-hearted efforts to push her cleaning mop. Pius nodded briefly back at her and walked over to the metal trolleys and containers which were neatly stacked along one wall. They seemed already prepared to take on the pre-cooked food for the flight home.

He stood staring at them for a moment. It seemed that this equipment was taken to the plane in a large metal container. He had seen these containers being loaded on and off before, both in Lagos and in London. He walked thoughtfully towards a double door which led out on to the tarmac. Standing on a trolley just beside this door was one of the large metal containers. He opened its door and peered inside. Quite big enough for a person to be squeezed into, he thought, especially if he was in a state which made him incapable of resisting. All at once something in one corner of the container caught his eye and he bent down and stretched inside to see what it was.

It was a piece of folded paper and as he opened it, he suddenly realised how he and Prince had been brought into the airport building undetected and unobserved. It was Bisi's note, the one she had tried to give to him at Lagos Airport.

'I hope to follow on next flight to UK,' he read. 'I will

contact you via our friend, Daniel, at H.C. I think I am on to something involving the crew of flight 800. I have seen Queen and am well informed. Bisi.'

He thoughtfully folded the note and put it into his pocket. He suspected that Bisi was right and that the crew of flight 800, or some of them, were in league with Samson Sigwe and Sung. But why? What for?

He walked slowly back into the service area. The Pakistani cleaner was still there, singing a mournful song in Urdu quietly to herself as she pushed her mop backwards and forwards, totally oblivious of time and space or even of the very surroundings where she was working.

He glanced round about him once more. In one corner of the service bay was a large metal door which he felt must be some kind of food store. He walked over and turned the handle – it was locked.

'They lock it,' the woman shouted over to him. She had stopped pushing her mop and was leaning on the handle. 'They lock it. You never get inside there. I never understand why they lock it.'

'What do you mean, you don't understand?' asked Pius walking over to her with a friendly grin on his face.

'There is nothing inside there except rubbish. I know, I seen it, I seen it.' The old woman was nodding her head up and down knowingly and grinning at Pius with a toothless grin.

'What kind of rubbish?' asked Pius. 'Why do they want to lock rubbish away?'

'I don't know,' said the old woman with a shrug. 'I never seen so much rubbish. Most people throw rubbish away, but not this Sunshine Airways.'

'Well, you never know with Sunshine Airways,' said Pius. 'The airline which produces the unexpected. It's my airline so I should know.' The old woman laughed and continued to push her mop.

'Still,' she said, 'they nice people. They always give me five pounds every time they land. That's why I am here now. I wait for the flight to come in so that old mama can get her five pounds.'

Pius looked at her in amazement. 'You mean every time Sunshine Airways flies in here someone gives you five pounds? What ever for?'

'To push away,' the old lady said with a knowing cackle. 'To push away. Not every day, mind you, only Monday and Friday. On those days they no like see mama cleaning here, so mama get five pounds to push away. Mama no fool.'

Indeed not, thought Pius to himself. So that's why the old woman pushes her mop back and forth on a clean floor. To kill time until the flight comes in so that she can collect her five pounds. But why was it only on two weekdays when the flights landed every day?

'They come soon,' the old lady continued. 'If you stay, maybe you get five pounds to push away, too.' This thought clearly amused her and she burst into uncontrollable laughter only stopping when she paused to wipe away the tears in her eyes with the end of her sari.

Pius glanced at his wrist-watch. The plane was due to land in ten minutes. In fact, if it was still ahead of schedule then it should be due in any moment. Somehow he had to ensure that he, too, was not pushed away. Today was Friday and he was determined to find out for himself just why the crew were so keen for the cleaning lady to leave the service area as soon as they disembarked.

'Hey, mama, I'll give you ten pounds to push away today. There's a real bargain for you!' The little old lady's eyes opened wide in amazement.

'Ten pounds? Are all you Nigerians crazy?' she asked.

'No, but I am just feeling generous. Take it and push away very quickly. If you stay on you will only get five from the flight crew.'

She snatched the money from out of his hand and tucked it into the upper folds of her sari. 'Mama go,' she said and picking up her mop and bucket left the room, shaking her head in amazement at the way she was treated by 'these Nigerians'.

Pius looked urgently round about him. The only possible hiding place was behind a long, orange curtain which hung down from the large plate glass window which looked out on to the tarmac. It was a highly dangerous place because he knew he could be seen from outside the building, but he could not see anywhere else which was more suitable. He had to get into the best possible position to see exactly what was going on.

The roar from a plane's engine left him with no time for further speculation. An aircraft had landed and seemed to be taxiing towards the Sunshine Airways' section of the airport. He could just make out the figures of three dark-uniformed airport officials who were already standing at the top of the tunnelled shoot through which the passengers would disembark. Flight 800 had arrived.

Moments later the plane had come to a halt and was connected to the disembarkation shoot. Five minutes after that the passengers started to disembark. Pius moved cautiously behind the long, orange curtain and wrapped it carefully round him, only too well aware of the precarious nature of his hiding place.

A door banged and moments later two crew members from flight 800 entered the service area. They were joking and laughing between themselves and Pius immediately recognised the tall air hostess who had hurled abuse at frightened passengers when they had finally settled down on the flight from Lagos. Her mood was very different now.

'Ah, Olu,' she cried out, struggling to contain her laughter. 'You are a good story-teller. That one was one of your best.'

Her companion, a smart, young man in an immaculate crew member's uniform, puffed out his chest at the compliment and put his arm around the girl's waist.

'Then there was this other passenger, now if I tell you what she did, why you will never believe it!' the man began.

'No, no, Olu,' the girl cried out. 'Not now. Save that story for another time. It is time we took something to eat.'

'OK, Rose,' said the man she called Olu. 'Let's see the delivery through and then go and find something. I thought tonight we might go out and see the town. How do you feel about that?'

'Suits me,' said the girl, putting her hand on his arm and giving it a squeeze.

Olu kissed her lightly on the cheek. 'Ah, Rose, life is good, eh?'

'Very,' said the girl. 'But the others will be here soon so leave the kissing until later.' She laughed again but she suddenly stopped abruptly as a large metal container, similar to the one in which Pius had found Bisi's note, was pushed into the service area by more crew members. Olu walked over to the container. 'This is the last one we do, Rose,' he said quietly. 'They will have to switch to another part of the world after this one.'

The girl did not reply but walked over to the large store and unlocked the massive metal door. As it swung open, Pius peered forward to try and see what was inside it.

'Right you two,' said Olu addressing the two cabin crew who had pushed the metal trolley into the room. 'Off and onload and make it quick.'

The two men opened the metal container. Its rear end faced Pius and try as he might he could not see what it contained. It appeared that the two men were removing dozens of small plastic packs in order to transfer them to the store. There seemed to be hundreds of them and the container took nearly fifteen minutes for them to unload it. Pius nearly gasped out loud in amazement when the men finally entered the store and then began to load the container with what appeared to be exactly identical packs.

'Quickly! Quickly!' said Olu, a note of urgency sounding in his voice. 'This is taking much too long.'

The two men struggled to complete the job. After ten more minutes the packs from the store were stored in the container and the container's packs were stacked in the store. The container was then pushed to one side of the service area beside the trolleys and smaller containers which were waiting to take on the food for the return flight to Nigeria.

When the container was in place and the store door firmly locked, Olu turned to Rose once more.

'Come, Rose, it's time for us to make our hay while the sun is still shining. Thanks boys,' he said, turning to the two junior flight-deck members. 'I'll see you are all right later.'

The two youths nodded at him and Olu took Rose by the arm and led her out of the area and towards the main airport buildings. Her laughter echoed down the corridor as Olu began to tell her another story about a passenger who had insisted on bringing a kerosene stove on to the plane.

The two junior crew members paused a moment as if

uncertain what to do. Pius, who was totally mystified by the scene he had just witnessed, waited for them to leave.

'Why doesn't he pay us now?' one of the men said angrily. 'He said he would see us all right, but you know at man. This year, next year, sometime ...'

'Never,' said his companion. 'You know something, Daro, we could make trouble for Mr Awoniyi if he doesn't pay us properly.'

'True,' said the other man without enthusiasm. 'But when he does pay the money is good.'

'How many times have we been paid?'

'Three.'

'And how many times have we done this thing for them?'

'Six.'

'OK, he owes us for three trips. That's a lot of money.'

'He said the big man is over here in London. That when he returns for tomorrow's flight he will come with all the money. Didn't he tell you that?'

'Sure he told me. But you know Mr Olu. Anyway, what shall we do tonight? I don't want to stay here. Let's go to that club we went to last week.'

'What that Burlington thing? That cost plenty of money, Daro.'

'Yes, but you remember those girls?'

'I don't remember much,' said his companion with a laugh. 'Not after twelve o'clock. After that I don't remember anything at all!'

Daro laughed and took him by the arm and started to lead him out of the service area. 'I tell you one thing, I have never seen you dance better. You were the talk of the town.' They both started laughing at their mutual reminiscences and walked out of the room and into the corridor.

Chapter Ten

Pius emerged cautiously from behind the curtain and looked round about him. The room was empty but he could hear the sound of voices not far away. He moved silently and swiftly towards the container which had been loaded with the goods from the store. He opened its door and was amazed to see that each plastic pack contained two small pots of ordinary airline pepper and salt. Pius was totally baffled. They seemed to have been removing pepper and salt pots and replacing them with other ones, he thought. Nothing strange about that. It must be a routine operation. But why separate the pepper and salt from the food trays? Surely they all went together on one tray. And why so many? They must be far in excess of the number of passengers! He reached inside and took out a pack of the pepper and salt pots. They were neatly wrapped in cellophane and seemed harmless enough. He shook them and they seemed to be full.

He was just about to open the cellophane and remove the two pots when he heard the sound of approaching footsteps. Not wanting to trust further his good luck which had lasted so far remarkably well, he walked quickly to the exit door and out into the corridor. He then broke into a run and made straight for the airport security inspector's office.

When he reached the office door he heard the sound of Prince's voice raised in argument from within. He held the door handle but stood still and listened.

'But I tell you you are utterly mistaken' Prince was saying. 'I did not enter illegally. I was brought in here under duress and in a drugged state.'

'That's what Mr Shale said. That's what your friend said. But that story is a pack of lies. I have a warrant here for this man's arrest and for the arrest of the other illegal entrant from Nigeria, Pius Shale. Do you two men understand me?'

Pius froze in horror. What was going on? He withdrew his hand from the door handle as the inspector continued.

'I want an immediate search put out for Shale who is somewhere in this airport. He must not leave. I suspect he is still in the vicinity of the Sunshine Airways service area.'

'Very good, sir. Will you alert all areas ...?'

Pius did not wait to hear anything further. The inspector was after him armed with an arrest warrant. He would be lucky to get out of the airport without being picked up and arrested.

He ran down the corridor and then down two flights of stairs which led into the passengers' lounge. Here he slowed to a brisk walk. A taxi and a good one was the only answer to this immediate problem, he said to himself. He ran down another two flights of stairs to the area where all the incoming flight passengers left the

98

building. There was a queue for taxis, stretching forty metres. Pius looked wildly about him, half expecting to see the approach of an army of policemen armed to the teeth and ready to shoot without compunction. He ran to the head of the queue where a middle-aged South American lady was struggling to load a mountain of luggage and badly tied packages into the leading taxi.

'Why, Mary!' shouted Pius. 'What are you doing here in London. How wonderful to see you!'

The Brazilian lady who had never in her life set eyes on Pius, stared at him in blank amazement as he grasped her and kissed her on both cheeks.

'I no speak ... I no be ...'

'Mary, Mary, this is so fortunate a meeting,' said Pius picking up her luggage and stowing it carefully aboard the taxi. 'Fancy meeting you again after all these years.'

'I never know ...'

Pius handed the taxi driver fifty pounds. It was pocketed instantaneously.

'You travelling with your friend?' said the taxi driver with a smile. 'If so, be quick before she changes her mind.'

Pius thanked his lucky stars that he had found someone co-operative. He stacked the last suitcase and then bundled the unfortunate woman into the taxi.

'But, but, but,' she protested. Pius slammed the door, the driver released the brake and the taxi moved away from the building.

'OK, mate. No funny business,' said the driver, turning round to stare at Pius. 'If you touch that lady I will throw you and your fifty pounds out into the road.'

'Don't worry,' said Pius. 'I am here for the ride, nothing more.'

The lady, whose knowledge of English was virtually

non-existent, started to shout out.

'Kensington Hotel. Kensington Hotel. Please take me. Now, now.'

'OK, lady. You sit well away from her, mate. The cheek of you people passes all understanding,' he muttered under his breath. 'It's enough to get us all thrown into jail. And where might you be heading?'

'Assembly Hall, Pinner,' gasped Pius.

'Pinner! It's going to be a very expensive trip,' said the driver firmly. 'Very expensive for you, mate.'

'I'll pay.'

'You'd better. We are going to Kensington first and I will see that you will pick up this good lady's bill too. Having terrified her out of her wits, it's the least you can do.

'Just get a move on and I will pay.'

The driver seemed to accept this and drove rapidly away from the airport. The Brazilian lady glanced nervously at Pius, but Pius was not in a mood for polite conversation nor for any smoothing down of ruffled South American feathers. He sat staring out of the window at the passing traffic, trying to work out just what had made the security inspector change from being a reluctant ally to an enemy at large. With the whole of the London Metropolitan police on the alert to arrest him for illegal entry he was going to be lucky if he wasn't heading straight for a police cell.

The lady was duly dropped down at her hotel. Pius thanked her but she had no idea what for. The taxi driver refused to take her money and pointed meaningfully at Pius. Then he drove off through the greasy, rain-washed streets of the suburbs of London and nearly an hour later they arrived outside a drab featureless building called the Assembly Hall, Pinner.

'One hundred pounds, mate,' said the man 'and that doesn't include the fifty first proffered. You wouldn't get many people taking a wild-eyed, young man like you on I can tell you. It's cheap at the price.'

Pius gave him his money and thanked him. He knew just how fortunate he had been to get away from the airport · so quickly. The driver might have been expensive but at least he had been co-operative.

Before attempting to enter the hall, Pius made for a telephone box which he had spotted on the other side of the street. Once inside, he dialled the home telephone number of Daniel Owusu.

'What you want, Pius?' said Daniel sleepily when the telephone was eventually answered. 'Can't you leave me alone out of office hours?'

'Listen,' said Pius. 'There is something very strange going on at the airport and it involves flight 800.'

'We suspected that,' said Daniel laconically.

'I know we did, but the only thing that I have found out is that they seem to be involved in smuggling pots of pepper and salt.'

'Are you serious?' said Daniel suddenly taking an interest.

'Sure, I am,' said Pius, 'I even have a specimen right here in my pocket.'

'Are you certain that is ordinary pepper and salt?' asked Daniel.

'Yes, at least I think I am. I haven't yet had time to open it and check.'

There was a silence. 'Anything else?'

'Yes, it appears that every security official and policeman at Heathrow airport is on the look-out for me. They are holding Prince for illegal entry and now they have issued a warrant for my arrest.'

101

'What have you done?' Pius felt that Daniel was not unduly concerned.

'I have done nothing. I was given a special pass by the inspector of the airport security police then when I got back he . . .'

Suddenly the coin-operated telephone cut out and Pius realised to his dismay that he had not got any further change. He cursed under his breath and went out of the telephone box. It looks as though I shall be ending up at our High Commission seeking diplomatic immunity the way things are going, he thought grimly to himself. He stood for a moment and stared across the street at the dirty red-brick building which was the Pinner Assembly Hall. The lights were on and he could just hear voices raised from within in cries and rhythmic chanting. He speculated on the chance of being able to get inside without violence. There appeared to be a man standing on guard outside the entrance, though from his position it was impossible to discover anything about him. He pulled out the pack of pepper and salt, fingered it gently for a moment, and then thoughtfully returned it to his pocket. No time to give it a closer inspection now, he thought, and started to move across the street.

The first thing he noticed about the man who was standing outside the Pinner Assembly Hall was that he was black. He hoped that this cultural bond would enable him to get inside without too much trouble. However, the man's first words were not at all encouraging.

'Hey, you. What do you want here?'

'I am a Milky Wayfarer. I have come to attend the meeting,' said Pius smiling broadly.

The man looked him up and down.

'Where are you from? I have never seen you before. Do you have your pass?'

'I am from Nigeria, and I happen to be the nephew of Mister Prince. I believe that my uncle is due to make a unique contribution here tonight.'

The man appeared unimpressed by this.

'I was never told that he had a nephew. Sorry, no pass, no entry. Those are my instructions and I don't intend to break them.'

'Listen, my friend,' Pius began, but the man paid not the slightest attention and turned his back on him.

Pius decided to try one last ploy before resorting to other more compelling methods which he knew would not only be risky but even dangerous. The danger lying in the probability that he would wake up in a police cell.

He brought the last of Queen's money out of his pocket – fifty pounds – hoping that it might just be sufficient to persuade the man to change his mind. Pius decided not to say anything but to walk up to the man and offer him the money. If he refused it then he would have to hit him, there was no alternative. He had to get inside the hall as quickly as he could. He tapped the man on the shoulder. As he spun angrily round to confront Pius, five ten pound notes were held up in his face and Pius tensed himself to strike. Either the man would react in an outraged manner, in which case he would have to let fly, or he would take the money from him. The man hesitated for a fleeting second, long enough for Pius to realise that his monetary inducement could work. He waved the notes once more and stared hard at the man whose face began to soften. He knew that he was winning this battle of wills.

'How much?'

'Fifty.'

The man took the notes and counted them.

'Go in and sit in the back row. Any trouble and I will come in personally and remove you. Pius mumbled his thanks as the man ran his hands inexpertly down his clothing in a search for a concealed weapon. Satisfied, he nodded his head towards the entrance and Pius slipped past him and through the swing-doors. A wave of fumes and heat which smelt faintly of human sweat completely engulfed him. He blinked a moment to accustom his eyes to the lighting and then quietly moved towards a bench at the rear of the hall. No one noticed him as he sat down beside an Asian man whose eyes were fixed ecstatically on a small figure in a bright yellow robe on a platform at the front of the hall. The figure of Mr Sung in the firm grip of his faith. For this was the closing session of the convention and Mr Sung was determined that it should be a memorable affair which would remain firmly in the minds of his religious devotees. The lighting had been cunningly arranged so that green and orange lights flickered on the figures on the platform, illuminating first the high priests and then the handmaidens who were sitting in two lines just behind their leader. Victor was dressed in white at his master's side and the predominant colour which flickered around Mr Sung himself was that of a vivid green. The congregation were chanting in unison with Mr Sung and all eyes in the hall were concentrated on his small, compelling figure.

'Our Father.'

'Our Father.'

'Lead us to the galaxy.'

'Lead us to the galaxy.'

'The source of power.'

'The source of power.'

Their voices droned on and Pius began to feel the sinister, hypnotic influence of Mr Sung gradually creeping over him. He forced himself to look away from the magnetic and powerful eyes which swept the hall from left to right – holding everyone in their compelling grip.

Suddenly, Mr Sung raised his voice.

'And now my fellow believers of the Gunk and spiritual disciples,' he cried, 'I will reveal to you the proof for which you have waited. The proof for which I know you have craved. My brethren, you will see this proof positive of my teachings. The visitation of that great spiritual mystic from Nigeria, Mister Prince.'

There was a murmuring from among the congregation and a sudden air of excited expectancy filled the hall.

Mr Sung paused for a moment and spoke to Victor who hurried off the platform, closely followed by two of the high priests. Minutes later they walked slowly back into the hall carrying between them the inert body of a man which they laid gently at the feet of their spiritual leader.

Pius stared in amazement. It was difficult to see clearly from where he was seated but the man lying so stiffly and silently in front of Mr Sung appeared to be dressed in clothes very similar to those of Mr Prince. Mr Sung raised his hands high in a threatrical gesture. The handmaidens started to hum a lilting tune and slowly lifted their arms above their heads.

From the highest point in the hall, the well-known voice of Mr Prince was heard quite distinctly and clearly.

'Greetings, brethren. This is Brother Prince speaking to you all. With you in flesh and in spirit but with the one

105

totally disunited from the other. My spirit is above you. My body lies before you as a living proof of the power of spirit travel and of our ability to reach our Gunk.'

'Our Father. Our Father.'

Some of the congregation started to beat their chests in an expression of ecstacy. The atmosphere became more and more electric as Mr Sung cried out.

'Power of the Gunk. Power of the Gunk.'

Pius felt himself swept up in the emotion and tried to overcome a powerful feeling of affinity with the people in the hall which was rapidly overwhelming him. He shook his head vigorously in a great effort to think independently. There was a violent disturbance behind him and suddenly he heard shouts and whistles being blown. Moments later a strong and authoritative voice sounded over a loudspeaker.

'Everyone stay exactly where they are. That is an order from the police who are here in considerable force.'

There was a gasp from the congregation who looked first at each other then at Mr Sung and finally round at the speaker at the rear of the hall. The hall itself suddenly filled with policemen. One of them had already put a restraining hand on Pius's shoulder.

'This is a police announcement,' the man continued. 'We have discovered that this organisation is involved in illegal drug-smuggling activities. No one may leave the hall until they have been questioned and cleared. Everyone on the platform is under immediate arrest.'

A group of armed police were forcing their way towards the platform and for a bizarre moment the voice of Mr Prince continued to run on with its pre-recorded message.

'Power to contact your Gunk in the galaxy. Power to

roam at will. Power . . .'

Suddenly Mr Sung made a dash for the exit door at the side of the stage. One of the policemen jumped up to give chase but Victor was too quick for him and brought his forearm down on the back of the man's neck. He dropped to the platform floor writhing in agony. Realising that the building was surrounded, Mr Sung sprang back to the centre of the platform and with surprising agility raised the stricken policeman to his feet and held him in front of him like a human shield.

'If you attempt to touch me. This man will die,' shouted Mr Sung wildly. 'Do you hear? I have a gun and it is positioned in the centre of his back.' He raised his voice again. 'I will leave the hall with this policeman as my hostage. If anyone attempts to touch . . .'

Some of the congregation were beginning to chant: 'Our Father. Our Father. Power to your Gunk. Power to your Gunk.'

Suddenly, one of the handmaidens who had positioned herself directly behind Mr Sung leapt to her feet and flung herself at the Chinaman. Using her knee and arm she brought him crashing to the ground where he struggled violently with the girl for a few minutes. Policemen jumped on to the stage and soon overpowered Victor and freed the struggling handmaiden who was none other than Bisi.

'Well done, Miss,' said the officer in charge when he reached the platform. 'But who are you? Technically you are also under arrest as a member of this organisation.'

'It's all right. It's all right. She is one of us and a special agent in my country's service.' Daniel Owusu had rushed forward through the crowd of policemen and was helping Bisi to her feet. Mr Sung who was nursing a broken arm as a result of Bisi's expert treatment continued to look wildly round about him.

'The high priests are the real criminals,' said Bisi when she had recovered her breath. 'The so-called handmaidens are just simple girls who have been sucked into a drug smuggling conspiracy. Those men are the guilty ones and I have enough proof to put them and Mr Sung behind bars for the rest of their lives!'

Pius had reached the platform and was staring at Daniel in amazement.

'Sorry, Pius,' Daniel said. 'We had to keep one jump ahead of you although you have done a very good job. We had samples of the salt and pepper pots analysed – one contained heroin and the other cocaine.'

Pius whistled out loud.

'But where is Prince? This drugged man here who is dressed like him bears no resemblance to the real Prince.'

'Prince is fine,' said Daniel, 'we had to get airport security to arrest him for his own safety just as we tried to get them to arrest you, unfortunately you slipped through the net. But you and Bisi put us on to the salt and pepper. Without that evidence we had nothing to pin on Sung and his criminal gang.'

Chapter Eleven

Two days later, Pius and Bisi were back at Heathrow airport together with Mr Prince, Daniel and a very grateful officer from Scotland Yard police station who was with them to see them off on their Sunshine Airways flight back home.

'I don't like it,' said Pius half-seriously. 'Travelling on flight 800 again gives me an uneasy feeling just thinking about it.'

'Don't you worry,' said Daniel, looking up and smiling at a couple of passengers who passed by with enough domestic and electronic equipment to stock a small shop. 'We have weeded out the bad eggs.'

'Bad,' said Bisi. 'They were rotten. They stank. Drug smuggling is one thing, but heroin and cocaine is quite another.'

'And all packed into salt and pepper pots. Diabolically clever when you come to think about it. A product of that evil Chinaman's mind. But the cleverest men make fundamental mistakes.'

'But where did the stuff go?' asked Pius.

'All over the world. Each high priest was in charge of his own territory. One came from India another from America, another from Japan. Drug pushers are not concerned with colour or creed, they just concern themselves with distributing their product.'

'And making money.'

'Yes, of course, money. These two drugs on the black market are worth thousands and thousands of pounds. They also kill quite a sizeable proportion of the world's population every year.'

'So the drugs were smuggled round the world disguised in airline packs of pepper and salt.'

'Yes. Sung only had to corrupt two or three crew or catering members of any airline and he was in very lucrative business.

'But he believed in the Milky Wayfarers,' said Prince speaking up for the first time. 'He might have used it as a cover for his drug smuggling activities but he believed in his religion.'

'Well, he might have done, Prince,' said Daniel. 'Once upon a time he might have done. But personally I don't really believe it. I think that he always intended to use religion as a cover for something far more sinister and lucrative.'

'Well, we are very much indebted to you all,' said the police officer from Scotland Yard. 'Even my colleague here at the airport,' he added with a laugh.

'Yes, he fooled me,' said Pius. 'When I heard him threatening to arrest me I thought he must be a crook as well.'

'He had to play a double game,' said the officer. 'He knew more than you realised and in fact believed you implicitly when you both said you were smuggled into the country in a drugged state. He had even got a lead on Sung and flight 800 but could not discover how they smuggled the drugs – until you turned up the pepper and salt. He was very nervous lest you should go charging in and getting into greater danger.'

'But why did he arrest Prince?'

'Well he was playing a very clever game. A double game in fact and had managed to convince the crew of flight 800 and indirectly Sung that he was harmless and incompetent. He arrested Prince for his own safety and Sung used another man dressed like Prince for use in the spirit travel routine. Sung had already made Prince record a message to convince the Milky Wayfarers when they had tortured him earlier.'

'So Airport Security had managed to infiltrate flight 800,' said Pius.

'They had been in touch with me and the High Commissioner all along because of the involvement of the airline crew officials,' said Daniel Owusu. 'They wanted to keep us fully in the picture because of the possible political embarrassment an arrest could cause.'

'It's a lucky thing that so small a number of Sunshine Airways staff are involved,' said Bisi thoughtfully, 'otherwise it could have been a political problem.'

'My real problem is that none of you believe me,' said Prince seriously. 'Not one of you believes that I really can do it.' Everyone looked hard at Prince.

'Do what?' asked Pius eventually.

'Spirit travel. If you want to take my body home then I will fly on ahead of you just to prove that what I say is absolutely true.'

'No you won't,' said Pius firmly. 'You are going to stay right where you are and get on that plane with me. Bisi has lent me her handcuffs and I intend to use them. I have taken out a business contract with your wife to return you safe, sound and in one piece. I intend to do just that. I am not letting you out of my sight for one minute. We are due to board flight 800 in twenty-five minutes and until we do...' The rest of his sentence was cut off by a voice on the loudspeaker directly above them.

'Sunshine Airways regret to announce that flight 800 has been delayed due to adverse weather conditions at ...'

Pius and Bisi looked at each other and suddenly burst out laughing.